CHASING THE FIRE

THE FIRST RESPONDER SERIES BOOK 6

JEN TALTY

JUPITER PRESS

This book is a work of fiction. Names, characters, places, and incidents are products of the author's imagination or used fictitiously. Any resemblance to actual events or locales or persons living or dead is entirely coincidental.

"*In Two Weeks* hooks the reader from page one. This is a fast paced story where the development of the romance grabs you emotionally and the suspense keeps you sitting on the edge of your chair. Great characters, great writing, and a believable plot that can be a warning to all of us." *Desiree Holt, USA Today Bestseller*

"*Dark Water* delivers an engaging portrait of wounded hearts as the memorable characters take you on a healing journey of love. A mysterious death brings danger and intrigue into the drama, while sultry passions brew into a believable plot that melts the reader's heart. Jen Talty pens an entertaining romance that grips the heart as the colorful and dangerous story unfolds into a chilling ending." *Night Owl Reviews*

"This is not the typical love story, nor is it the typical mystery. The characters are well rounded and interesting." *You Gotta Read Reviews*

"Murder in Paradise Bay is a fast-paced romantic thriller with plenty of twists and turns to keep you guessing until the end. You won't want to miss this one..." *USA Today best-selling author Janice Maynard*

CHASING THE FIRE

FIRST RESPONDERS SERIES BOOK 6

NY Times Bestselling Author
JEN TALTY

BOOK DESCRIPTION

Eloise never believed she needed love until its dangled in front of her and then nearly taken away in a fiery blaze.

Dr. Eloise Porter has worked hard to become an emergency medical doctor. She has no time, or inclination for romance. Not even for Rick "Edge" Honor, the sexy firefighter/paramedic who has an uncanny ability to make her smile, even on the darkest of days.

Edge doesn't take no for an answer very often and he doesn't give up easily. He's determined to get the sexy Eloise Porter to go out on a date if it's the last thing he does. It takes some doing, but he finally wears her down. While their budding romance heats up, so does a series of suspicious fires, all targeting urgent care facilities, doctors offices, and emergency rooms. Determined to keep his doctor friend safe, Edge puts himself in the line of fire only to create a perfect storm that will put his life, and hers, in grave danger. He'll be able to save Eloise, but will he be able to save himself?

A NOTE FROM THE AUTHOR

The First Responder Series is a spin-off series from my *NY State Trooper Series*. Neither series needs to be read in order. Frank Harmon from **Dark Water** and Reese McGinn from **Deadly Secrets** make a cameo appearance in this book.

Also making a guest appearance is Cameron Thatcher. We first meet Cameron in **Legacy of Lies** as a secondary character. Cameron has his own book, **Secret Legacy**, which you can pre-order now.

THURSDAY AT SEVEN IN THE EVENING...

*R*ick Honor, or better known by everyone as Edge, climbed down from the cab of his brand-new shiny pickup truck and meandered across the parking lot toward Blue Moon. A bunch of his fellow firefighters were meeting inside for drinks, some bar food, and some good live music. Edge had lived in the Lake George area for about six years and never wanted to leave. It had to be the most beautiful place on earth.

And with the nicest people ever.

It made keeping his promise to his late wife a lot easier.

"Edge. Fancy meeting you here," a familiar woman's voice said from somewhere behind him.

He closed his eyes briefly and slowly turned

when what he really wanted to do was ignore Dr. Tamara Blossom. She was nice enough, maybe. But she wasn't the doctor Edge wanted to spend his time with. Not even close.

"Care to join me for a drink while I wait for my friend?" Tamara asked.

"Sorry. I can't." He looked around for his buddies, grateful to make eye contact with one of them. No one could ever call Edge a coward, but when it came to Tamara, not only was he tired of turning the woman down, but he was frustrated with the idea she hadn't gotten the hint yet.

"Hey, Edge. Over here," Troy Farren, one of the younger, single firefighters at the station, waved from a table where he sat with Damien Bryant. Again, about ten years younger than Edge, and also single.

Which was nice.

However, it made Edge feel like an old man, but sometimes hanging out with the men who were his age got tiresome because they were married, with kids and that was something Edge just didn't need in his life right now.

"I'm late meeting some guys from the station," Edge said.

Tamara curled her fingers around his biceps and

smiled. "Maybe when you're done with them we can have share a nightcap." She batted her fake lashes over her dark eyes. There was no doubt that the woman was pretty, but she tried too hard, and it made her look fake.

Which was kind of funny since her personality couldn't be more inauthentic.

"I've got to work tomorrow." He shrugged.

"How about when you get off, I make you a good home-cooked meal."

He let out a long breath. He knew what it was like to be rejected a million times, but he'd finally taken the hint and decided that he wouldn't pursue Eloise anymore. She wasn't interested, and he had to respect that. Why couldn't this woman take no for an answer?

"Tamara, you're nice lady. But you and I are never going to happen. I'd appreciate it if you could stop trying to get me to go out so I don't have to keep turning you down. I don't want to hurt your feelings, but—"

"Oh my. I think I've given you the wrong impression this time." She patted his chest. "I just wanted to talk to you about something personal, and I thought it would be neighborly if I cooked you a meal."

"That's not necessary, and truthfully, it sounds like a date and again—"

"Edge, I'm sort of seeing someone now."

He blinked. She made no sense at all. If she was seeing someone, why the hell did she want to cook him dinner? "Oh. Well, I'm happy for you, but I don't think it would be a good idea for me to come over. That might give your new guy the wrong idea."

"He's not like that, but I would like to pick your brain about buying a boat."

He coughed. There were so many other people who had a hell of a lot more knowledge than he had regarding all kinds of boats. "I barely understand the one I have."

"Would it be okay if I called you?"

She could, but he wouldn't be answering. "Sure. Now I have to get going. Have a nice evening." He blew out a puff of air. He hoped he had never come on to Eloise that strong, and at this point, he was happy to be friends.

He glanced around and was pleasantly surprised to see Dunn Manning and Parker Jameson. Both worked at the fire station. Both were single, and both men were much closer in age.

Edge pulled up a chair on the outdoor patio just

as Parker and Dunn showed up with a round of beers and a bowl of popcorn.

"So, you decided to grace us with your presence," Dunn said.

"I didn't have anything better to do this evening." Edge glanced around the table while all his buddies stared at him with smirks on their face. "What?"

"We all saw that exchange with Tamara," Damien said. "Do you think that Eloise doesn't want to go out with you because of Tamara?"

Edge laughed. "Eloise asked me once if I liked Tamara, and I nearly spit out my soda. She knows I'm not interested, but the problem is, Eloise says she doesn't have the time to date." He shrugged. "I think that's a brush-off."

"Only a little bit," Dunn said.

"What does that mean?" Edge glanced over his shoulder. Tamara had disappeared into the crowd.

Thank God.

"Eloise had a bad breakup a long time ago," Dunn said. "She's been guarded ever since."

"And you're just telling me this now?" Edge rolled his neck. He'd all but given up on the sexy doctor.

"It's not my place and I don't even know the details," Dunn said. "But it might explain why she keeps shooting you down when it's painfully obvious she's got the hots for you."

"I wouldn't go that far." However, because Edge and Eloise both lived on Harmon Hill, both renting in the same duplex, they saw each other a lot and had become friends. Making it harder for him to stay away.

But he had stopped asking her out. He'd crashed and burned and now it was time to let the good doctor go.

"Then why did I run into the two of you having coffee in the village the other day?" Troy asked.

"And didn't you take her for a boat ride and a picnic on her rare day off a few weeks ago?" Parker asked.

Edge shook his head and laughed. "We live next to each other, and even though she's made it clear she's not interested, I'm not going to ignore the lady. Why can't a man and a woman be friends without everyone thinking it's weird?"

"Because we've all seen *When Harry Met Sally,*" Dunn said.

"I haven't." Troy furrowed his brow, looking all confused and indignant. The poor boy hated it when he missed out on something and everyone at work enjoyed picking on him.

"We can watch it at the station," Edge said. "Now, let's change the subject and have a good time."

"Here's to the singles' club." Parker raised his beer.

Edge clanked the longneck his buddy had given him and took a swig. He honestly didn't want to drink to that sentiment, but it was the truth. He was single. His heart skipped a beat. He missed Tina. So much so that sometimes it physically hurt. But she'd want him to keep moving on with his life, and that was exactly what he was trying to do.

"I don't know about you all, but I'm not ready to be in a serious relationship," Damien said. "But my mom sure is ready for me to be, and she keeps trying to set me up with all her friends' daughters. Sometimes that's really weird because I dated some of them in high school. One of which I'd lost my virginity to."

"That's kind of pathetic and embarrassing." Edge laughed. "My dad used to tell me if he was twenty years younger, he'd try to steal my wife, and there were times I thought Tina might be keen on that idea." Edge missed his dad as much as he missed his late wife. His old man had been a strong constant in his life. His best friend. The one person he could always count on, no matter what. His mother had come and gone, and currently, he didn't even know where she was or what she was doing.

And honestly, he wasn't sure he cared all that much. Hell, she didn't give much of a shit about her only kid, so why should he care?

Only he did.

More than he wanted to admit.

"You want awkward? How about that my folks are trying to fix up Troy with my sister Emma." Damien shook his head. "And Troy over there doesn't seem to be trying to squash that effort with either of our families."

"Not to mention he's flirting with her all the time at the station," Parker said.

"I am not." Troy leaned back and folded his arms across his chest. "I've known Emma my entire life. We're just close friends."

Damien waggled his finger. "And you better keep it that way."

Troy would not be able to keep that in the friend zone, especially since a person would have to be blind not to notice that Emma had the hots for Troy. Eventually, those two would be a couple, entangling the Bryants and the Farrens once again since Echo Farren married Spencer Bryant, a fellow firefighter.

Station House 29 was more than a fire department. It was a family, and that was a literal statement as many of the firefighters and paramedics were related.

"Your sister can date anyone she wants," Damien said. "And that would include me." He arched a brow. "If that's what she and I both wanted, but we don't so it would be nice if everyone would just leave us alone."

Troy laughed, raising his hands. "That sounds like a man who's a little bit interested."

Edge leaned back, sipping his beer, and glanced around the patio. The crowd was pretty thick for a Thursday night. There were a few couples on the dance floor, swaying to a slow country song. It reminded him of a time in his past where he thought he was happy. No. He'd been so blinded by love he couldn't see straight. It was a feeling he missed.

In his mind, he was meant to be the other half of a couple. He turned his gaze to the lake. It was a calm night. Not a single ripple rolled across the water. Tina had helped him take care of his father. His cancer had been aggressive, but his father hung on for months. The last few weeks of his life, he wasn't the man that Edge had admired.

Two weeks after he buried his father, his wife

found out she had breast cancer, and it had metastasized. And it was aggressive.

She fought like a real trooper, and the doctors did everything they could, but it wasn't caught early enough, and Edge blamed himself for that. Had she not rescheduled her mammogram a half dozen times because of helping him care for his father, they would have known the lump wasn't a fibroid and maybe she'd still be here.

His heart swelled remembering her last words.

I love you, Edge. But if you stop living, I'll come back and haunt you and it won't be pleasant. I beg you. Don't grieve for me too long. You deserve to find love again, and you know you'd want me to. So go and do it. I demand it.

She closed her eyes and held his hand. She passed two hours later.

He turned his attention back to his buddies. "Is anyone going to order food besides me?"

"Hell yes," Dunn said. "Parker is in charge of food for our next shift, and he's the worst in the kitchen."

"Screw you," Parker said with a chuckle. "Now I'm going to sneeze in your muffin."

Edge waved the waitress over and the table ordered an assortment of appetizers and a couple of buckets of seltzers.

The new beer.

That's what Eloise called them, and she was right. A lot of people were switching to them and just about every beer company had produced their own spin on the alternative alcoholic beverage.

"What's up with you tonight, man?" Dunn poked his forearm. "You're being unusually quiet, even for you."

Edge might be reserved in social situations, but he wasn't the kind of man who kept his emotions to himself. When he'd first come to Lake George and people would ask him about his past, he never hesitated to tell them about his tragic losses. Talking about Tina helped him keep her alive in his heart. It also helped him focus on avoiding his promise, something he could no longer do and not just because it would upset Tina.

His wife knew him better than anyone, and he wasn't cut out to go through life as a single man. Yet he still found himself needing to discuss his past. He believed it gave him courage to move forward.

However, he learned that many people didn't appreciate his openness, but that's how he got through it. As a kid, he talked to his dad about every-thing, and his father always told him real men shed tears. And that feeling things to his core and sharing them was never a bad thing, and Tina always said that's why she fell head over heels in love with him the second they met.

"My mind is wandering," Edge said. "My dad and Tina would have loved it here."

Dunn squeezed his shoulder. He'd lost his father two years ago to a massive heart attack. "My dad always wanted to see Niagara Falls. He figured when he retired, he'd do it. He used to always say it wasn't a long drive so he just kept putting it off."

"Have you ever been?" Edge asked.

"We were going to make it a boys' trip." Dunn snagged a seltzer from the ice bucket and cracked it open. "My brothers and I are planning to go next year around the anniversary of his death. I know it will be hard, but it will be good too."

"That's a nice way to pay homage to your dad," Damien said. "He was a good man."

Everyone raised their cans.

"To our dads," Parker said. "And to Tina."

Edge took a long swig. None of these men had ever met Tina or his old man, so for them to include both in a toast meant the world to Edge. It helped him keep moving forward like both would have wanted.

"Hey, Troy. There's your brother Morgan. And in uniform." Damien pointed across the room. "I still can't believe he came off the mountain and got married."

"No one saw that coming," Troy said. "Especially our family, but now that Morgan's settled down, my mom has moved on to the rest of us and it's annoying as hell."

Morgan nodded as he paid for a takeout order. He snagged his bag and made his way toward the table. "What a motley crew."

"How's trooper life treating you?" Parker asked.

"I can't believe I'm going to say this, but I love it." The radio on Morgan's uniform crackled.

"All officers in the vicinity of the Village Urgent Care Facility, please respond to a 10-79," the dispatcher said.

Edge stiffened his spine.

Morgan tilted his head, bringing his mic closer to his lips. "Sergeant Farren responding. ETA less than ten minutes." He let go of the mic. "I have to run. I'll see you later." He turned on his heel and bolted through the crowd.

Eloise was working at urgent care this evening.

"I'm out of here." Edge stood and dropped forty dollars on the table. "Let me know if I owe more."

"You can't do anything," Dunn said. "You might as well sit tight until we hear more."

He understood they wouldn't let him in the building or be part of any investigation. He wasn't on duty, and a 10-97 was a bomb threat, not really a firefighter's specialty unless the damn thing went off. "Maybe not. But I'm sure Eloise is shaken up and could use a friendly face."

"She's lived here her entire life. Everyone is a friendly face." Parker cocked his head.

"Well, one more won't hurt." Edge wasn't going to stand there and argue with his buddies over the fact that Eloise had made it pretty clear she preferred Edge as a friend. He pulled his keys from his pocket and made a beeline for the parking lot.

His heart pounded, and his chest tightened. While he'd promised himself he'd get over his feelings for the sexy doctor, knowing she could be in danger only brought all those intense emotions to the surface.

He eased out into traffic and did his best not to drive like a madman. It took him nine minutes to get to the urgent care facility and another three to find a parking place since it was filled with fire trucks and police cars.

He raced toward the barricade.

Morgan and Frank, another state trooper,

stepped out in front of him, blocking him from going any further.

"You can't go in there," Frank said. "It's an active situation."

Edge scanned all the bystanders. "Where's Dr. Eloise Porter?"

Frank and Morgan exchanged a glance.

"She's inside," Morgan said a little too calmly.

"Why?" His eyes widened when he saw the bomb squad enter the building in full gear. "And don't lie to me."

Morgan squeezed his forearm.

Edge didn't think that was a good sign. He resisted the urge to shrug it off.

"The facility received a call that a bomb had been left in the doctor's office. That it was under the chair and if anyone sat on it and then got up, it would trigger the bomb to go off."

"Jesus. Are you telling me that someone is sitting on an active bomb?" Edge asked.

Frank nodded.

"And next, you're going to tell me that person is Eloise."

"It is," Morgan said, squeezing harder.

"Fuck." Edge yanked his arm free and took three steps to the side.

Frank grabbed his arm and pulled him back. "Don't make me restrain you. Let the bomb techs do their job."

"Who the hell is in there with her?"

"Do you know Reese McGinn?" Morgan asked.

"The owner of the Heritage Inn? Yeah. I've met him a few times." Edge planted his hands on his hips and sucked in a deep breath. "He used to be a trooper, right?"

"Fucking good one too," Frank said. "I hated to see that man leave. But more importantly, he was in the Marines and has some experience with explosives."

"He's a civilian, and you let him inside?" Edge folded his arms. What he really wanted to do was bolt right past his friends and into that building.

"He was already inside with one of his kids who has an ear infection. When he learned what was happening, he sent his kid outside with one of the other patients until his wife could get here." Morgan pointed across the street where a large crowd had gathered. "And he stayed inside to help keep Eloise calm and check out the bomb."

A man who looked like Reese stepped from the front door.

"Looks like they kicked him out." Edge swallowed. "I want to talk to him."

Frank glanced over his shoulder. "Reese, can you come here for a second?"

Reese nodded. He waved to his wife and held up a finger, indicating he'd be there in a minute, and then he jogged over to where Edge stood. "What do you need?" Reese ran a hand through his hair and let out a puff of air.

"You remember Edge," Morgan said.

Reese stretched out his hand. "I do."

"How's Eloise?" Morgan asked, not wanting to do small talk.

"She's holding up really well," Reese said.

"And what do you know about the bomb?" Edge asked.

"It's relatively simple, which is good and bad." Reese glanced over his shoulder before turning his attention back to Edge. "The problem is it's got a double trigger."

"What does that mean?" Edge knew about fires, not bombs.

"Once she sat in the chair, the extra weight engaged the bomb. So, if a certain amount of weight is released, the bomb goes off," Reese said. "But the bomb was also practically built into the chair, so the only way to disarm it is to get into the seat, and that will take some doing."

Edge rubbed the back of his neck and started to pace.

"Relax, Edge," Morgan said. "You know we've got an excellent bomb squad. She's going to be fine."

"I hope you're right." Out of the corner of his eye, he saw Eloise being escorted out by one of the bomb techs, who was no longer wearing the top part of his suit.

"Are you going to keep standing in my way, or will you let me cross this line?" Edge stared at Morgan.

He took a step back. "Just stay out of everyone's way, and if you're asked to leave, do it."

Edge barely heard him as he raced toward Eloise.

2

THURSDAY AT SEVEN IN THE EVENING...

*D*r. Eloise Porter closed the exam room door and took a long breath. Thursdays weren't supposed to be this crazy, but so far, since she clocked in this afternoon, it had been one patient after another with not even a bathroom break.

And dealing with Nathan Blossom only added to her high level of stress.

She pulled open the door and left it open. She glanced over her shoulder and nodded at Mindy. She needed someone to be a witness to this conversation because it might not be received very well. "Nothing's broken," she said. "I can give you an anti-inflammatory for the swelling and that should help take the edge off the pain as well. Make sure you keep icing it on and off too. All of that will make a big difference."

"But it hurts like hell, Doc." Nathan rubbed his shoulder and arm, making a face. "I need something stronger. This has been an ongoing issue for me."

"I can't give you pain pills." She signed the piece of paper and handed it to him. "Not for this. You don't need them."

"Come on, Eloise. My regular doctor would call it in. I'm in so much pain from past injuries; you have no idea."

"Then maybe you should have your general doctor paged." Eloise knew for a fact that his doctor would never prescribe this man pain medication unless he was near death. "I'll walk you to reception."

"Don't fucking bother. I can see myself out," Nathan huffed. "Thanks for nothing." He hopped off the exam table and shoved past her, nearly knocking her into the wall.

She groaned, contemplating calling security. She took in a deep breath and counted to ten, thankful when she heard him mutter a few more obscenities under his breath before making his way out the door.

"He's a piece of work," Mindy said as she scooted by to clean the room. "Tamara's going to be pissed he was here, and then she's going to be mad you didn't treat him with more kindness and maybe a couple of pills. That's what she's told others to do."

"Please. He's lucky I don't call the cops, and if she keeps doing that, she'll lose her license to practice medicine."

"She never does anything except help others find reasons her brother needs them."

"He does have a plethora of injuries from his time in the military. I don't doubt the man is in pain, but he's addicted to drugs. He needs therapy, not someone enabling him."

Her cell buzzed in her pocket. She pulled it out and stared at Tamara's number on the screen. Wonderful.

"Hello?" she answered.

"Um. Hi, Eloise. My brother said he was just there with a broken arm and you—"

"It's not broken."

"I see," Tamara said. "He says he's out of his prescription and needs just a few pills to tide him over until he sees his regular physician. I can't write him that script."

"Nor can I," Eloise said. "I'm shocked that you'd even ask."

"No. I understand. I simply wanted the full

picture and your side of the story. Thanks for being honest," Tamara said. "Have a good night."

The phone went dead.

"See how she backpedals," Mindy said. "That's how she covers her own ass."

Eloise let out a long breath. "Tamara needs to stop this insanity with her brother. It's going to get her in a shit ton of trouble one of these days."

"She never crosses that line," Mindy said. "She only asks to see if others will. When they won't, she backs off. Fortunately, her brother is now out of options at this facility."

"Hopefully, he doesn't have anyone else willing to prescribe them. But now he'll turn to the street, and who knows what kind of crap he'll find there." She needed five minutes before the next patient. Her back ached and her feet throbbed. She'd done a night shift at the ER yesterday, only to get about four hours of sleep before heading to the urgent care facility where she'd not only do her four-hour shift, but another four hours for Dr. Tamara Blossom. It wasn't that Eloise minded. Not at all. She had student loans and other bills that she needed to pay, not to mention the avoidance of having any kind of social life. And the only way that would happen was if she worked her ass off.

Her cell buzzed again.

She groaned and then smiled. Edge had a way of making her heart beat just a little faster.

Edge: *There was a package for you on the porch. I brought it into the shared foyer. Along with your mail.*

Eloise: *Thank you. Much appreciated.*

Edge: *What are neighbors for? I have a twenty-four-hour shift tomorrow, but if you still want me to install the soft-close brackets in your kitchen, I can do them on Saturday.*

Eloise: *Only if you let me pay you.*

Edge: *It's really not necessary. But if you insist. I prefer to be paid in your homemade cookies. Or pies. Or cakes. I don't discriminate.*

She laughed. When she became really stressed and couldn't sleep at night, she'd bake. It always helped her relax, more so than anything else. And when she did, she'd only have a nibble or two, but since she'd learned to bake at a large bakery where they did things in bulk, she didn't know how to make just enough for one, so she ended up leaving them for Edge to take to the firehouse.

Eloise: *That can be arranged. Thanks.*

If she were to ever be interested in going out with a man, it would be with someone like Edge. He was all man, but he had a soft, cuddly side that made her heart melt. He'd suffered some great losses, and yet, he lived his life with a glass half-full attitude.

For some reason, she suspected he might have gotten that from his late wife.

She really enjoyed spending time with Edge, but it wouldn't be fair to start anything with him, or anyone else for that matter. Until her career was exactly where she wanted it, and she had her debt cut in half, she wasn't going to become sidetracked by a man.

No matter how cute or charming.

Of course, even the thought of dating brought up some emotional battle scars she wasn't sure would ever go away and that scared her because it had been five years since Larry had ripped her heart out and changed her forever.

She tucked her cell back in her pocket and entered the nurses' cubicle. "I'll be in the office for a few minutes. I'll be in to see the next patient in about five," Eloise said.

"I'll put them in exam four." Mindy, the nurse, handed her some paperwork that needed to be signed. "I'll let them know it might be a few more minutes."

"For a Thursday, it's been a crazy evening."

"At least we close at ten tonight." Mindy adjusted her stethoscope.

Eloise would be able to go home and sleep all night, for a change. That was a rare treat. She opened the door to the office all the doctors used and tossed the paperwork on the desk while staring at a new chair. It was much nicer than the last one, and she wondered how it fit into the budget.

That had to be the work of Dr. Tamara Blossom. Tamara managed the facility, but sometimes she did things that made no sense to Eloise. However, the old chair had to be the most uncomfortable thing in the world. Half the time, Eloise would sit out in the nurses' area to do her work because every time she sat in that stupid chair, it wouldn't stay at the height she wanted.

She eased herself into the big executive leather seat and sighed. "God, that's nice. Thank you, Tamara," she whispered as she leaned back and closed her eyes.

"Don't sit...shit." Mindy skidded to a stop at the door.

Eloise leaned forward.

"No!" Mindy held out her hands. "Don't move a muscle." She waved her cell. "The police are on their way."

"Excuse me?"

"Someone just called and said there was a bomb under the chair in the doctor's office," Mindy said with tears rolling down her cheeks. "Reese McGinn will be back here in a second to—"

"I'm right here." Reese owned the Heritage Inn, one of the best family resorts on this side of the lake. He was also a former Marine and an ex-trooper. He lowered himself to the floor. "Eloise, you're going to have to remain very still."

"Is there really a bomb under my seat?" She gripped the armrests and held Mindy's gaze while Reese lay on the dull tile floor.

"Mindy," Reese started. "You need to make sure everyone is out of this building and then stay out. When the police get here, tell them what's going on, but I don't want anyone in this building except the bomb techs."

"I can't leave—"

"You have to," Reese interrupted. "Go. Now." He moved to a sitting position and placed a hand on Eloise's knee. "I'm not a bomb expert, but I have a lot of experience with them from my military days and from what I can tell, the bomb was engaged the moment you sat down. If you even get up just a little, it might go off."

"This is not making me feel any better." She swallowed. Hard. Hoping her body didn't even shift a centimeter.

"The good news is I don't see or hear a timer, which means as long as you don't get up, we could have all the time in the world."

"Still not helping." She breathed slowly and methodically, keeping all her movements as minimal as possible. "Shouldn't you be leaving too?" Not that she wanted him to, but she couldn't be responsible for anyone's death.

"I will when the bomb techs get here."

"If you blow up, your wife is going to hate me," Eloise mumbled.

"Patty knows what's going on, and I'd be sleeping on the sofa if I left you here by yourself." He ducked his head under the seat again.

"Any way to defuse the damn thing?"

"Shall I keep being honest or do you want me to sugarcoat things?"

She swallowed. Hard. "I prefer if you shoot straight from the hip."

"The bomb seems to be part of the seat."

"What the hell does that mean?" She blinked. Her heart lurched to the back of her throat and then dived into her stomach with a twisted splash. She couldn't fill her lungs, which was probably a good thing because that might cause her to move too much, which would then cause her guts to be splattered across the room.

"The part of the device that I'd need to get at is inside the cushion." He shifted to his knees. "I don't feel comfortable fucking with it by myself." He caught her gaze. "I hear sirens. They will be here shortly and they will figure this out."

Tears burned her eyes. "This is a new chair."

"Since when?"

"Today," she said.

"Who bought it? Who put it together?"

"I have no idea," she admitted. "It was here when I got to work. I'm going to assume Tamara ordered it, but she hasn't worked in three days." One of the perks of doing the schedule was that Tamara didn't give herself too many shifts, especially weekends or nights.

"The police will need to know when it arrived and who was in charge of assembling it. They are also going to need—"

"Are you doing my job again?" Morgan Farren stepped into the doorway.

Reese stood. "Just being a good citizen."

Morgan bent over and glanced under the seat. He

stood and raked a hand across his head. "Can you continue being a good citizen for a bit longer while I help Frank with the press and the crowd? The fire department just arrived, and the bomb techs are about five minutes out."

"I didn't plan on leaving until they were here." Reese gave her a slight nod.

A tear rolled down her cheek. Of all the ways she could leave this world, this was not one that she'd ever imagined.

"It's going to be okay, Eloise," Morgan said. "We're going to get you out of here safely." He stepped back into the hallway and disappeared.

She glanced at the clock on the desk and only ten minutes had passed since she found out about the bomb. But it seemed like an hour. She blinked out a couple more tears. She wanted to wipe them away but was too afraid to move her hands from the armrests for fear she might explode.

The sound of multiple footsteps in the hallway hit her ears like sweet music.

Reese stuck his head out the door. "The bomb team is here." He turned. "They are going to make me leave. Is there anything you need for me to do before I go?"

"Why were you here to begin with?"

"I think my one-year-old has an ear infection."

"When I get out of this chair, let me take a peek in her ear. We've got sample antibiotics here in the office."

He nodded as some man wearing a large funny suit pointed.

Reese waved. "I'll see you shortly."

"I'll hold these guys to that."

"Just try not to move unless we tell you to," the man in the big protective suit said. "I'm Justin. And that guy over there is Allen. We'll get a good look at the device and go from there, okay?"

She nodded.

"Allen. I need to cut into the cushion."

Eloise didn't really want to hear a blow-by-blow. She closed her eyes. Not a good thought.

"You see that?" Justin asked.

"That's easy-peasy," Allen said. "Cut the red wire first."

"And what happens if you cut the wrong wire?" she asked.

Allen glanced up. "That's not going to happen."

"Red one is cut," Justin said. "Now, let's weigh this sucker down and get her out."

Allen stood in front of her. "I'm going to place my hands next to your right leg, and as I press down,

I want you to slowly climb over me. Can you handle that?"

She nodded like a freaking bobblehead.

"Ready?"

"Yes," she whispered.

"All right. Here we go." Allen placed his hands next to her right thigh. "Shift to the left. Slowly."

Holding her breath, she shifted.

"Good. Keep going," Justin said. "I've got the lever now...wait. Don't move for a second."

She froze.

"I can see the other wire now. I'm going to cut it," Justin said. "And the bomb is now disarmed." Justin lifted her from the chair and set her on her feet as he removed the top part of his suit. "You're okay. The bomb can't go off now."

For the first time since she sat down, she sucked in a really deep breath. "Can I go outside?"

Justin smiled. "Yeah. Let's get you out of here." He guided her through her own office and toward the front door.

The tears came fast and hard as soon as the warm summer air hit her face.

"Eloise." Edge's voice tickled her ears. She glanced around until she found him jogging in her direction.

She took off running and threw herself into his arms and started sobbing.

"Hey, there. You're okay now. I'm here. I've got you." He wrapped his arms around her and held her close.

She nuzzled her face into his neck. "I was so scared."

"I know. So was I," he whispered as his warm, tender lips pressed against her temple.

She sunk into his strong body, digging her fingers into his shoulders. She wasn't sure her legs would support her much longer.

He cupped her face. "But it's over now and you're safe." He brushed his lips gently over her mouth. It wasn't a very long kiss, but it certainly was a powerful one, and the second he broke it off, she shivered.

"I need to find Reese," she said.

Edge arched a brow. "To thank him for staying with you?" He brushed a piece of her hair behind her ear.

"Kind of." She ran her hands across his shoulders. "He was there because his little girl had an earache and I want to make sure I examine her before they leave."

Edge rubbed his thumb across her cheek. "You're always thinking about everyone else."

She smiled. "I could say the same thing about you."

"I guess it comes with our careers." He rubbed her forearms. "I think Reese is across the street with Patty and the kids. I know the police are still going to want to talk with you. I'll stay until all that is over and we can go home together."

"You don't have to do that."

"I don't want you driving home alone, especially since we don't know who put that damn thing in there, or why." He took her chin with his thumb and forefinger. "And until I know that it wasn't directed specifically at you, I'm your personal bodyguard whenever I can. I'll try to switch some of my—"

She covered his mouth with her palm. "You will not. I won't let you."

"You can't control my actions." He smiled and winked. "And seriously, wouldn't you feel better having me around until we know what that was all about?"

She inhaled sharply and let it out slowly. "Yes," she said softly. "But I don't want you taking time off work. My schedule is insane, and you can't follow me around the hospital, which has security guards."

"You let me worry about my job and keeping you safe."

She had no energy left in her body to argue. Besides, she didn't like the idea of being alone. She'd let him hang around until whoever did this was caught and behind bars.

3

*T*entatively, Eloise entered the urgent care facility.

"Please try not to touch anything," Morgan said. "This entire place is a crime scene now."

"How long will it have to be closed?" She shivered. Not only could she have died, but her staff and all the patients waiting to be seen. Had Mindy not stopped her, the carnage would have been horrific.

"It will take until tomorrow morning for our team to dust for prints and look for clues. After that, I doubt it will be more than a day or two before we can allow you to reopen, but don't quote me on that. I'm not the man in charge. This is now a federal case and the FBI will be taking the lead. An agent by the name of Cameron Thatcher."

"As in Jacob Donovan's old partner?" She put on the gloves that Morgan handed her before finding a few things she needed to check inside little Ambrose's ear. Eloise used her key to find a sample of antibiotics.

"That's the one. He's young, but Jacob says he's the best."

"I trust Jacob, so if he says so, it must be." She snagged her doctor's kit and backpack. "This is all I need for now. Has anyone gotten ahold of Tamara?"

Morgan nodded. "She's on her way, if she's not already outside." He glanced over his shoulder. "We're only letting you back in as a favor to Reese."

"I understand, but I doubt Tamara's going to be happy. She's going to want to come in and see what happened. She's a bit of a control freak when it comes to this place."

"I've heard that from Mindy. She says that Tamara is a pain in the ass to work for sometimes." Morgan stood in front of the door. "But that lately, Tamara's been taking some time off."

"I forget Mindy's your cousin." Eloise wasn't one to pay attention to or participate in gossip. "I've been taking some of Tamara's shifts. I don't mind. I think she's secretly seeing someone because she's been weirdly happy and I know she wants to be married and have a family."

"I don't know about that. I just saw her at the Blue Moon and she was a bit flirty with Edge." Morgan pushed open the door.

"She's like that with everyone. Even women. It's weird."

He laughed.

"Do I need to go to the station or something and make a statement?" She stepped outside, grateful the crowd had dwindled down. Reese stood by the fire truck in the parking lot, holding his one-year-old little girl. His wife, son, and other daughter were sitting on the back while Edge and a couple of his buddies entertained the two children.

Edge was so good with kids it was crazy. She'd never seen a single man who could get down on a child's level so easily and quickly.

"For now, we have everything we need. However, the FBI will want to have a chat with you."

"Thanks for everything, Morgan. I really appreciate it. Say hello to Lizzy for me."

"Just doing my job." Morgan squeezed her forearm. "Tamara is here and she's with a man." He pointed across the lot.

"Any idea who that is?" She squinted. The dark

night had been lit up by all the flashing red lights from the police and fire vehicles. "I don't think I know him and I know everyone in this town."

Morgan did a double take. "Are you kidding me? You don't recognize your ex-boyfriend?"

She blinked a few times and tilted her head. "Holy shit. I can't believe that's Larry." She rubbed her forearm. "I haven't seen him in nearly five years. He swore he'd never come back to Lake George. What the hell is he doing here?"

"I have no idea, but it looks like Cameron is about to have a chat with her," Morgan said. "I'm going to have a listen. Stay safe."

"I will." She strolled toward Edge, Reese, and his family. Her heart still raced wildly out of control. Her blood pressure was probably through the roof. She inhaled slowly and deeply through her nose and let it out in a big puff from her mouth. She did this three times in hopes it would calm her nerves.

Ambrose had her little thumb in her mouth while she rested her head on her daddy's strong shoulder. Her cheeks had a pink glow, which made Eloise think the little girl had a slight fever.

"You really didn't have to do this," Patty, Reese's wife, said as she hopped off the back of the fire truck.

"It's the least I can do considering what Reese did for me." She handed Edge her doctor's bag. She dug inside and found a digital forehead thermometer. "Hi, Ambrose," she said softly. "I hear you're not feeling well."

The little girl snuggled deeper into her father's embrace.

"I'm just going to wave this over your head." The thermometer beeped a few seconds later. "She does have a touch of a fever." Eloise handed the instrument to Edge, and she pulled out an otoscope. "This isn't going to hurt."

Reese bent down a bit.

Eloise tugged at the side of Ambrose's ear and took a quick peek.

She squirmed and started to whine.

"All done," Eloise whispered. "Well, your assessment was correct. She has an ear infection."

"This is her third one in two months." Patty picked up her other daughter. Her son ran over to his dad and hugged his leg. "My other kids never really got them."

"Here's an antibiotic for her, but since she's had that many in a short time, you might consider taking her to a specialist. I can recommend someone if you want."

"That would be awesome," Reese said. "We really appreciate it."

Eloise curled her fingers around his biceps. "I owe you my life. I wish I could repay you."

"You just did." Reese leaned in and kissed her cheek. "Be safe."

"I'm taking her home." Edge pressed his hand on the small of her back. "I plan on being by her side as much as possible."

"Frank said they would be increasing patrols?" Eloise tilted her head.

"They did. But they can't be parked at the top of our driveway day and night," Edge said. "So, we'll need to coordinate our schedules."

"I don't want you to change your world for me."

"Eloise!" Tamara rushed over. "Oh, my God. I was so worried." Tamara waved frantically as she raced across the parking lot.

Larry one step behind.

Freaking wonderful. He was the last person she ever wanted to lay eyes on again. Talk about a jerk. What she ever saw in him, she couldn't remember because he'd ruined any good thoughts she'd ever had about him when they'd broken up.

"We better get going, babe," Patty said. "These kids are tired."

"If you need me for anything, you know how to reach me." Reese stretched out his arm and shook Edge's hand.

This was, in part, one of the reasons Eloise never really left the area. She went as far as an hour south for her undergraduate degree and then chose to attend Albany Medical School. Being able to stay close to home and her family, what little of them were left, had meant the world to her, and now she got to serve the community in which she grew up.

Life couldn't get any better than that.

That was until an ex-boyfriend showed up.

"Holy shit. Are you sure you're okay?" Tamara flung herself at Eloise, hugging her a little too tightly. As if she actually cared all that much.

Eloise took a step back. She wasn't used to that kind of affection from anyone, but especially not from Tamara. They were barely friends, and while Eloise respected Tamara as a doctor, she wouldn't socialize with her outside of work. "It was pretty scary, but I'm fine, in part thanks to Reese."

"Glad to hear that," Larry said as he stuffed his hands deep in his pockets. His gaze shifted anywhere but on her, fucking coward.

She stared at him for a moment. He'd cut his hair short, which was one of the reasons she hadn't recognized him. She hated to admit it, but he looked. Damn good.

But he'd always been a handsome man. He could even be charming when he wanted to be. However, they were over for a reason.

"We were at the Blue Moon when I saw Edge race out. I knew something had to be going on, especially when his buddies left shortly after. But I had no idea it had anything to do with the urgent care facility. I can't believe someone put a bomb in that new chair." Tamara spoke so fast her words were mushed together. "As I told that FBI agent, I wasn't even here when it came in. I'm not actually sure when that was since I took a few days off. But I did pay extra to have it put together. Where's Mindy? I bet she knows when it was delivered. Did she speak to the police?"

"She did," Eloise said. "And the chair was already assembled when we got to work today, so she didn't know."

"That's weird." Tamara glanced around. Someone would have to sign for it, and we have a policy that all packages must be logged. Did anyone check that?"

"No one added it," Eloise said. "I showed the police the records and it wasn't there."

"Well, the security cameras will tell the police a lot," Edge offered as he slipped his arm around Eloise's waist, pulling her closer. "If you don't mind, I'd like to take Eloise home now. It's been a long night for her."

"You don't have to do that," Tamara said. "Larry and I can take Eloise home. We have to pass her place to get to mine."

"I have my own car." The last thing Eloise needed was to spend any time with her ex. "I can drive myself."

"If you want to leave it, you can. We can always get it in the morning," Edge said. "Or, I'll just follow you home."

"And who are you?" Larry asked as he puffed out his chest.

"I'm Edge. A friend of Eloise," Edge said, not offering a hand. "And you are?"

"Larry. An old friend," Eloise muttered, not wanting to get into the logistics of all of it. "Thanks for the offer, Tamara, but Edge lives on Harmon Hill too. It's no trouble for him to follow me."

Tamara narrowed her eyes, crinkling her fore-head. "Oh. That's right. You two are neighbors. I keep forgetting that."

"When did you move there?" Larry asked. "What happened to buying that—"

"Larry, my life is no longer your concern." She let out a long breath. She shouldn't have been rude, but she didn't have the bandwidth to deal with Larry.

Or Tamera for the matter.

"Here comes Cameron," Edge said, thankfully interjecting before she said something she might regret. "Excuse us." He gave her a little nudge toward the center of the parking lot. "You're going to have to explain him to me," Edge said with a tinge of humor dripping from his words.

"He's not worth my breath."

"Except your body is one big ball of tension and while it's been like that since you stepped from that building, it got a million times worse when he showed up." Edge massaged her shoulder.

She could feel the knots forming.

"Are you Doctor Eloise Porter?" a young man flashing a badge asked.

"You must be Cameron Thatcher." She smiled. "I've heard a lot about you from Katie Donovan."

Cameron chuckled. "She has better things to say about me than her husband, which is funny since he's the one I used to work with." He took out a small notebook. "I've spoken to everyone that was in the facility and got a detailed description from Reese from what he saw. I just need to ask you if there is anyone you can think of that would want to hurt you."

She pointed to herself. "Me specifically? You think this was meant for me and not anyone and everyone in the facility?"

"We don't know. But since you were the doctor in the building, we have to look at that as a possibility. So, have there been any patients, or family or friends of patients, or anyone you can think of that is holding a grudge or angry about something you did or didn't do?"

"Not that I can think of." She glanced toward the sky, searching her brain for any workplace conflicts. She was an emergency room doctor, and she saw a lot of trauma, and oftentimes, people yelled at her or became impatient with their level of care. But nothing that stuck out where someone would want to kill her. "I've never been threatened by a patient or anything."

"What about a loved one who had someone die and blamed you?" Cameron tapped his pen on his pad.

"That's never happened that I'm aware of," she said.

"What about that guy back there?" Edge asked.

"What guy?" Cameron said.

"The one that came with Tamera." Edge arched a brow. "Which is weird to me for different reasons."

"My ex-boyfriend? Larry Greyling?" She swallowed the bile that smacked the back of her throat when she let her lips say his name. "He doesn't live in the area. I didn't even know he was back. We haven't spoken in five years. We have a history, but not one that would include him wanting to blow me up."

Cameron glanced at his notepad. "According to his girlfriend—"

"Please don't tell me he's dating Tamara," Eloise interrupted.

"He is and he's moved back to the area," Cameron said. "So, was it a bad breakup?"

"It was a long time ago," she said. "We didn't see eye to eye on a few things, like moving back up here when I was done with medical school. He also had a wandering eye. Not necessarily a big deal since it appeared he only looked, until one day it wasn't his eyes doing the wondering, but his hands. More than once. And I caught him. He thought I'd forgive him since we'd been together since high school, and I thought about it until I found out he'd been cheating on me on and off our entire relationship."

"When was the last time you spoke with him and how did that go?" Cameron asked.

She shrugged. "Probably a few weeks after I dumped him, and I told him to go screw himself. That I never wanted to see him again. And he respected that, and this is the first time I've seen him since."

"You're certainly still angry," Cameron said.

She blew out a puff of air. "I didn't expect to see him, much less with someone I know, and I want to tell her to run for the hills, but also, I was just sitting on a bomb. My bedside manner is a little off."

"Fair enough," Cameron said. "Do you have a business card? If not, would you mind writing down your contact information?"

She took his notebook and scribbled her address and cell.

"Here's my card." Cameron handed her one as well as Edge. "If you can think of anything that might aid me in this investigation, please let me know."

"Will do." She nodded.

Edge stepped in front of her and took her by the biceps, rubbing up and down. "I don't mean to pry, but something tells me there is more to that story between you and Larry."

"I don't want to talk about it here, okay?"

"If there's more and it can help—"

"It can't. But it's embarrassing and very personal. I don't want to get into here." And maybe never, but for now, she'd put it off and when she got home, she'd be too tired to talk about it. "I just want to go back to my house and wash off the day."

4

*I*t was rare that Edge ever asked anyone to take a shift. Usually, it was him covering for his fellow firefighters. Especially the ones who were married and had children. So when one of his buddies was willing to switch around the schedule so his shifts were better in line with Eloise's workload, some of the weight on his shoulders had been lifted.

However, his concern over who and why the bomb had been placed in that particular urgent care facility couldn't be squashed until they found the bastard that had done it, and Morgan said they had very few clues.

Other than whoever set the bomb up had a more than an average understanding of explosives.

He stepped from his kitchen with a plate of homemade nachos and a glass of red wine. He knew it was an odd combination, but he didn't care. He didn't feel like a beer, and he didn't have much to eat in the house, so this would have to do.

He set them on the coffee table in the small family room of his second-story, one-bedroom apartment. He glanced out the big picture window. A half-moon hung high in the sky while bright stars glistened on the lake below. A small boat hummed down the shoreline. All he could see was the vessel's lights and the white waves it made.

His late wife would have loved visiting Lake George. It was one of the reasons he choose this place to settle into his new normal.

As he made himself comfortable on the sofa, he turned his head and stared at the door that led to the staircase, which connected him to the downstairs apartment where Eloise lived. Her place was a two-bedroom and twice the size, but he didn't need anything but a place to rest his head.

Besides, he liked the view of the lake.

Only now, he worried about Eloise being on the first floor. He'd tried not to scare her about how vulnerable she was as he went through her place, securing the windows and making sure the security system was working properly. He also tried not to ask too many probing questions, but Larry gave off a strong vibe, and he didn't trust him.

He picked up his tablet and Googled Larry Greyling.

A bunch of articles, images, and videos popped up—all about Larry and his tech company and the products his company sold. It appeared that the man had made a few million dollars right out of the gate, and his company was doing extremely well. There didn't seem to be any bad press regarding anything. The dude looked like a stand-up guy.

However, Edge was never fooled by appearances.

A tap at the door startled him and he sloshed some wine onto his lap. "Shit." He swiped at his thigh with a napkin before he jumped to his feet and paused midstep.

He blinked, taking three large strides toward the door. He curled his fingers around the lock, twisted, and yanked open the door. "Are you okay?" He pulled Eloise into his apartment. "Did something happen?"

"I'm fine." She raised her shaky hand and tucked some hair behind her ear.

"You don't look fine. You appear positively

shaken up." He helped her to the sofa. "What happened?"

She pointed to his wine. "May I?"

"Go ahead." He'd get another glass in a second. He did his best to be patient while she took a few sips, but something had rattled her nerves, which in turn, made his curious brain go down a twisty road that wasn't a joy ride.

She leaned forward and set the glass back on the table. "I couldn't even sit in the family room and not worry if someone was watching me."

"That's a shitty feeling."

"It sure is," she said softly. "I wanted to take a shower, but all I could think about was the movie *Psycho*."

He covered his mouth.

"I'm glad I amuse you." She fell back on the sofa. "I went into my bedroom and locked the door, but then I heard a little noise. The wind picked up and the leaves rustled, making me jump. A car whizzed down the road, which made me scurry to the window to see if that vehicle continued or came down Harmon Hill. Floor boards creaked, and I realized that was you walking around."

"I'm really trying not to be so heavy-footed, but it's a family trait."

"Actually, that noise wasn't so bad because it made me feel like I wasn't alone." She turned her head. "But then my phone buzzed. I haven't spoken to that asshole in five years, and now he has decided to text me."

"What did he say?" Edge had a million other questions he wanted to ask, but this was a good start.

"It started off innocent enough, asking me if I was okay and if I needed anything."

"Personally, I still find that suspicious because he's your ex and the time that has gone by since your last communication," Edge said.

"Well, it got weird when he asked me not to tell Tamara about his past. He says he's changed and got help for his problem. Obviously, she knows he and I were an item. Everyone who knew us in high school or college knew that. But she thinks we broke up because I was too absorbed in my future career and didn't have time for him, which is untrue. Well, not totally, but he didn't break up with me. I'm the one who called it quits, but I believe he's telling her something different. He likes to weave this story about how I would dangle the marriage carrot in front of him and we'd talk about buying that old run-down house on Rockhurst next to the Bateman estate."

"That's for sale? I didn't know that," Edge interrupted. "That place has some serious potential."

She shook her head. "It's not on the market. I know the owner and they have talked about selling for the right price, and to the right people, whatever that means. However, Larry loves to tell people that I would talk a big talk but I would never commit to him and that's why we broke up. Only that's utter bullshit. It's not even remotely what happened, but I honestly don't care and I'm not going to go around and correct people. It was five years ago."

"But it's got you're tailfeathers ruffled now," Edge said. "Why?"

"Because he's asking me to lie to Tamera." She rolled her eyes. "I could almost get on board with that because she makes me crazy for different reasons. However, I feel like I'm being played, and she's being used, and while I don't like her that much, I feel like I can't let this one thing go."

Edge shifted in his seat and snagged the glass of wine. He couldn't help but wonder what kind of game Tamera might be playing in all of this, but he'd save that question for later. "What did he do that pissed you off and made you dump him?" Being direct didn't always win him brownie points, but something told him that this Larry guy was more than a rich, cocky asshole.

Eloise groaned. "God, this is so embarrassing. You're going to think the worst of me."

"Impossible." He smiled. "Whatever it is, I'm sure it's not the first time two people broke up over it."

"Maybe not, but it doesn't make me feel any better." She squeezed her eyes closed. "He recorded us having sex and didn't tell me." She blinked, scrunching her face like she'd just ate a lemon.

He coughed red wine onto his lap. "Shit," he mumbled. "That is so not cool."

"It gets worse."

Edge downed the rest of the wine and set the empty glass on the table. He wasn't sure how anything could get much worse than that. "I'm listening."

She covered her face with both hands.

He decided there was no reason to force her to look at him while she told this story. He could certainly understand why she'd want to bury her face in the sand.

"I found out about the video because I caught him jerking off to it."

Edge lowered his chin and arched a brow. "Seriously?" He tugged at her hand, pulling it from her face. "At least it was to you and not someone else."

She waggled her finger. "One would think that; only, he was on one of those video chat things, and some girl was watching it with him while she was shoving a vibrator, you know where."

His jaw slacked open. He'd heard and seen some weird things in his life and this one was right up there. "I'm speechless."

"So was I. So much so I stood there staring at him doing this for a few minutes before the girl on the screen told him that someone was standing behind him and started laughing and saying something about the look on his sexy girlfriend's face."

"Can I ask who this girl was?"

"The only thing I know about her was that he met her on some sex chat website, and he often shared pictures of me that he'd take while I was sleeping or in the shower. It was a game he played with her, and she shared pictures of her and her boyfriend. It was disgusting. I was utterly mortified. For all I know these images and videos are all over the web." She groaned, tossing her arm over her eyes. "I spent the first year after we broke up scouring the internet for my image. I never found anything, so I let it go. But now I'm freaking out again."

"I don't blame you, and we should tell Cameron about this."

"Oh, my God. No," she whispered. "I've never told anyone but my therapist."

"Yeah, well, I'm sure he's heard worse. Seen worse. I mean, I could tell you a few strange stories of where men have stuck their privates, and I being a first responder, have had to—"

"I know all about those. Have you forgotten I'm the ER doc you brought them to?" She pursed her lips.

"Good point."

"Yeah, it's totally embarrassing for those men. But this felt like a violation."

"It was." Gently, Edge lifted her arm. "You didn't do anything wrong. Larry did."

"I know that, but it doesn't make it any less humiliating."

He laced his fingers through hers, rubbing his thumb over her soft skin. "I understand why you'd feel that way. I'm sorry that happened to you. Do you think he's asking you not to say anything because he's the one who is embarrassed, or because he doesn't want to get caught again?"

"He says he's changed," she admitted. "I mean, he had a lot of remorse when I found out, and he came up with a few creative excuses."

"I wish I could say I don't want to know the excuses, but curiosity killed the cat."

"Bottom line was he said he got pulled into this weird world, and it became addicting, and now he's saying he's a different man. That he's been in therapy and doing well."

"It sounds like you had a conversation with him, not just a simple text."

"Only text messages. I don't actually want to speak to him outside of when I saw him tonight."

"I wish you hadn't done that," he said. "Can I look?"

"Sure." She pulled her cell from her back pocket, unlocked it, and handed it to him.

He quickly scanned the short conversation. The man had all but begged Eloise not to say anything to Tamera. He'd stated that while he would always be tempted to go back to that lifestyle, he spoke to a therapist once a week and avoided as many triggers as possible.

The messages themselves seemed benign. Satisfied it wasn't anything too horrible, he handed her the phone back. "Don't erase those, and you'll have to tell Cameron about this. It could be important. Your ex-boyfriend is a pretty smart guy, from what I read on the internet about him."

"He's a lot of things, but I doubt he'd try to kill me, especially after five years."

Edge had to agree. It did seem like a long stretch of time to wait. "Perhaps. But I still want you to call Cameron."

"Can it wait until the morning?"

"Of course." He leaned forward and snagged a chip loaded with cheese. It was cold now, but he didn't care. "Want some? Or want more wine?"

"No, thanks," she said, letting out a long breath. "However, I do have a huge favor to ask."

"What's that?"

"You're going to think I'm crazy."

He leaned back, wrapping his arm around her and pulling her to his chest. "I already think that, so you can't make it worse."

She laughed. "I can't sleep downstairs alone. Would you mind sleeping in my guest room?"

"I've got a better idea." He tilted his head. "Why don't you stay up here? I'll take the couch and you can have my room. It's got a great view of the lake."

"I don't want to kick you out of your own bed."

He arched a brow. "You were doing that by

asking me to crash at your place. Besides, I end up falling asleep on the sofa most nights. It's not a big deal and we're both up here. I've got an extra toothbrush in the bathroom." He stood, taking her hand. "Let me walk you to your accommodations, ma'am."

"Oh, my God. You're so weird."

"It's been a long night."

She palmed his face. "Thank you. You've been a really good friend to me."

Friend. Not exactly what he wanted, but it was better than nothing. "Did you lock your door?"

She nodded.

"All right." He waltzed into his room and grabbed a pair of shorts and some clothes for the morning. He found his spare sheets and a blanket and took one of the pillows off the bed, which he hadn't made. Heat rose to his face. "I washed the sheets two days ago, so they are basically clean."

"Thanks. I'm sorry to—"

"Don't think twice about it." He kissed her cheek. "If you need me, I'll be right out there on that sofa." Turning on his heel, he made his way back out into the family room. He set his bedding on the sofa and picked up the empty wineglass and the nachos he didn't really get to eat.

As he cleaned off the plate in the kitchen, he

contemplated having another glass of wine to help him sleep, which was going to be impossible with Eloise tucked away nice and neat in his bed.

The vision in his head wasn't helping any.

He set the dish on the drying rack and stared out the window. That's when he saw movement.

A shadow slinked across the sideyard. He flicked off the light to get a better look, but whoever or whatever was out there had disappeared into the woods.

He quickly shot off a text to Morgan. Hopefully, whoever was on duty tonight was close by. Edge was tempted to go outside, but if someone was out there, he didn't want to leave her vulnerable and alone.

Morgan: *I'm two minutes away. I will walk around and check things out.*

Edge: *Thanks.*

He tucked his cell back in his pocket. Shit. He'd left his charger in his bedroom. Wait. He had left one in his kit, which was hanging in the bathroom. He twisted the knob and pushed in the door. He blinked, staring at Eloise wrestling with her shirt to pull it down over her half-naked body. "Oh, crap. Sorry." He tugged the door closed. It was time to fix the damn lock.

Crash.

Bang.

"Ugh," she said.

"I'm coming in." He pushed the door open and tried not to laugh, but that proved impossible.

She'd fallen backward into the tub, with her shirt still over her head. At least the shower curtain had covered her breasts.

Not that he didn't like what he saw, but he was sure she hadn't meant for that to happen.

"Let me help." He leaned over the tub and pulled the fabric down past her face.

She quickly wiggled, making sure the shirt was properly in place while he managed to untangle her from everything else that had landed on top of her.

He helped her to her feet. "Are you okay?"

"I'm sure I'm going to have a bruise on my ass." She rubbed her fanny before pulling her shirt down. "I was going to take a shower, but maybe I should wait until tomorrow."

"Give me five minutes, and I can have this curtain rehung."

Her cheeks were about as bright red as a fire truck. "Thanks, but you don't have to do that."

"I don't mind." He sidestepped her and held up the rod. "Besides, this is just one of those cheap retractable ones." He made sure all the hooks were over the metal part before placing it between the two walls. "And there you go." He took a step back.

"That was very sweet of you."

"Do you want me to get anything from your apartment?" His cell vibrated. He glanced at it and frowned.

"What's wrong?"

"Morgan wants to talk to me. He's in our driveway."

She hugged her middle. "Do you think he found something?"

He wasn't going to tell her about seeing something outside. Not right this second. "Maybe. Why don't you take your shower, and I'll go see what he wants."

"I don't want to be here alone."

He placed both hands on her shoulders and squeezed gently. "You're not alone and I'm just going to talk to him on the side porch. No one can get up here without going through that door."

"Or scaling the siding," she said softly.

"You watch too many movies." He brushed his mouth across her soft, plump lips. "You're safe. Trust me."

"Right. And you just walked in on me half naked. And I thought I locked that door." She planted her hands on her hips and cocked her head.

"You probably did, but the lock is broken. I'll fix it tomorrow so this doesn't happen again."

"You're being awfully presumptuous to assume I'm going to spend another night up here."

"One can always hope." He pointed to the small linen closet. "There are extra towels and soap and stuff in there. I'll be back up shortly."

"I'll be waiting. I want to know what he said."

Edge nodded, snagging the keys from the counter. "I'll lock the doors. Hopefully, that will make you feel safer."

"It does, actually. Thank you."

He jogged down the staircase. "Hey." He stepped outside.

Morgan sat on the steps, and he glanced over his shoulder. "Took you long enough."

"Sorry. I was helping Eloise with something."

Morgan smiled. "She's upstairs with you? Nice."

"It's not like that," Edge admitted. "She just got spooked and didn't want to be alone, so I'm sleeping on the sofa and...no idea why the fuck I'm explaining this to you." Edge joined Morgan on the steps. "Did you find something?"

"I don't know," Morgan said. "When I pulled up

to Harmon Hill, I noticed a car about half a mile past the turnoff."

"That's about where this house sits if you're coming north."

"I was." Morgan nodded. "So, I kept going, and that's when I saw someone jog around to the driver's side and get in."

"Please tell me you pulled them over."

"Of course I did. And it was a punk named Scott Pinder. He's been picked up a few times for possession before marijuana became legal. I asked him what he was doing on the side of the road, and he told me he'd just stopped by his girlfriend's house to drop something off."

"Why did he park on the road instead of driving to the house?"

"Because his girlfriend's family hates him so they met in the woods. His story checks out, but I will keep an eye on him and talk with his probation officer."

"If that was him, why was he running through my yard?"

"I don't know, but he was shitting his pants when I pulled him over. He thought the girlfriend's father called the cops."

"Have you talked to the girlfriend or the dad?"

"I did. The problem is Scott is twenty-one. Angie, the girlfriend, isn't seventeen yet," Morgan said. "The father is ready to toss Scott under the bus if he comes around his daughter again, but so far, he can't prove anything has happened, and Angie swears they've never had sex."

"I hope for her sake they haven't," Edge said. "Maybe now that young man will walk away because that's a felony."

"Anyway, I wanted you to know what was going on." Morgan pushed himself to a standing position. "I've got to get going. My wife would like to see me before she falls asleep."

"I appreciate everything."

"My pleasure. Stay in touch." Morgan climbed behind the steering wheel of his trooper vehicle.

Edge wasn't sure if he felt better about what he saw or not. But for now, Eloise was safe. Hopefully, she'd enjoyed her shower and was climbing between his sheets.

He groaned. That was not a visual he needed stuck in his head.

5

*E*loise stuck her head out of the bedroom door and peered into the family room, half expecting to see Edge still asleep on the sofa.

Only, he was nowhere in sight.

Not that it mattered. She tugged on the hem of her shirt and took in a deep breath.

The bitter aroma of a fresh pot of coffee hit her nose. "Oh, God. That smells wonderful."

"I thought I heard you." Edge appeared from the kitchen, holding two mugs of coffee.

She jumped. "You scared me."

"Sorry." He handed her a cup. "If memory serves me correctly, you like a little cream and sugar."

"I do. Thanks."

"I'm making some breakfast. Are you hungry?"

"I'm starving," she said as her stomach growled.

"Come on back." He turned. "It's nothing special."

She set her mug down at the small table in the tiny kitchen, which was about half the size of hers and that wasn't very big either. "What are you making? I can smell syrup and cinnamon."

"I put together a little French toast bake my late wife used to make all the time."

"She sounds like she was a real sweet person." She sat up a little taller. He'd talked about Tina a few times and his eyes always lit up like a Christmas tree. But she could see an element of pain behind the obvious love he had for his wife and that saddened Eloise.

She understood loss. When her mother died a few years ago, it hit her super hard and to this day, she missed her mom so much it hurt her heart. And her father was still struggling to get on with the business of living.

"She was." Edge pulled out a tin and set it on top of the stove. "You two would have liked each other." He set a plate in front of her along with some real maple syrup. "Whenever we had company, she always made this dish. I almost never have company, so it's been a few years since I've made it. Hopefully, it doesn't suck."

She leaned over, letting the steam from the decadent-looking meal hit her face. She inhaled sharply. "Oh. That is just amazing." She snagged a fork and dug in. She let her head fall back and she moaned as she chewed slowly. "I think I just died and went to heaven…Oh shit. I'm sorry."

"Don't worry about it. It's just an expression." He smiled. "I'm glad it turned out okay. I'm not a very good cook." He joined her at the tiny table.

"How long were you married?"

While he'd talked about his late wife many times, Eloise never asked him questions, so she only knew a few fun facts and stories he'd shared willingly.

"About seven years." He shook his head. "She was only nineteen and I was twenty. The world thought we were crazy."

"That's young. What made you decide to get married?" She sipped her coffee and stared at him while he shoveled food in his mouth.

He waved his fork in the air. "Tina was pregnant."

Eloise's jaw slacked open. "I didn't know you had a child."

"I don't." He lifted his mug and took a long sip. "Our baby was stillborn at seven months."

"Jesus. I'm so sorry."

For as long as she'd known Edge, which was

going on three years since she moved back to the area, he'd always been open about his life and his past, but this was something he'd never brought up before.

He wiped his lips with a napkin. "A lot of people thought we were going to fall apart and end up divorced over it simply because that is what pushed us to get married, though we would have anyway. I know that to be a fact."

"You loved her very much."

"I'd been in love with her since the fourth grade." He nodded. "We decided to wait to try to have another baby in part because we were so young, but also because she had school to finish, and I was working crazy hours to make all that happen. We were trying when we found out she had breast cancer."

"That's rough." She reached across the table and placed her hand over his. "I'm truly sorry for your loss."

"Thank you." He squeezed her hand. "Most ladies I'm trying to date find it uncomfortable when I talk about Tina. I hope that's not why you've turned me down so often."

She tilted her head. Her heart fluttered. She'd never met anyone quite like Edge before. His honesty was refreshing and while she often didn't like people to be overly blunt, on him, it was an excellent look. "That's not why I won't go out with you."

"Would you mind enlightening me? Because I really like you and a couple of times I've wondered if you might feel the same way too."

She swallowed the thick lump that formed in her throat. Liking him had never been a problem.

However, after Larry, she not only didn't trust men, but she'd never allow herself to become dependent on any man.

Ever again.

"To be honest, it's not you."

"What do you mean?" He leaned back in his chair and held her gaze.

It was a bit unnerving, and she wasn't sure how truthful she wanted to be, except that she should tell him the truth. Not only was there no reason not to, but she liked him, and if she was ever going to move past what happened, she needed to be an open book with the one man she actually wanted to spend time with. "Because of Larry, I have trust issues with men."

"I can understand that."

Her brows shot up. That wasn't the response she

expected. Most people would try to explain to her why it was ridiculous and she should get over it. Her father had raised her to be the kind of woman who got right back on the horse that tossed her.

Only, every time she became intimate with a man, she found herself paranoid to the point she couldn't even enjoy sex.

And then there was the financial situation. Sometimes, that was more embarrassing than the actual sex tapes.

"You seemed shocked that I can comprehend that his deception had a lasting effect on you."

"Not shocked," she said. "But most people would agree that after five years, I should have been able to move past it."

"There's no timetable on when people should or shouldn't get over something. What he did was cruel and it hurt you. I'd be guarded too."

"This is going to sound crass, but how long did it take you to want to get back out there?"

"Tina made me promise her two hours before her last breath that I wouldn't sit around and mourn her forever. She wanted me to go find love again. She wanted me to have all the things she and I couldn't, and then she told me that I'd want the same for her, which is most definitely true if the tables had been turned." He lowered his gaze to his cup as he played with the handle. "The first year all I wanted to do was drink myself into a stupor, but all I could ever see when I closed my eyes at night was her disappointing glare." He shook his head. "I moved here about a year after she died, and I don't think I really started dating until two years ago, but let me tell you, it kind of sucks."

She laughed. "I've tried dating a few times, but to be fair, medical school was a nightmare, and then residency wasn't much better. Now, I need to make enough money to pay off my school loans, which is why I'm working at urgent care centers on my off days."

"You're burning the candle at both ends." He stood, clearing the table. "So, what you're saying is that I still have a shot."

She watched his muscles flex as he scrubbed the dishes while she contemplated lying. "Yes. You do."

He tossed the dish towel over his shoulder and turned with a wicked smile on his face.

She burst out laughing.

"I'm so glad I can amuse you." He folded his arms. "And since I have you smiling and laughing, how about we go out on a date tonight?"

"I have to work in the emergency room tonight."

"Tomorrow night?"

"You're not going to give up, are you?"

He shook his head. "You just told me that I still have a chance, so I'm like a kid who was given twenty dollars and left to his own devices in a candy store."

She pushed the chair back and grabbed her coffee. It took her four strides to cross the kitchen. Butterflies flapped about wildly in her gut. Flirting hadn't been something she came by naturally, even before Larry.

However, being around Edge, it flowed from her body like the sun rose in the morning every day. Whenever she saw him, she promised herself she'd keep it light and friendship based. She'd been relatively successful, and he'd been super respectful of her feelings, even after she'd told him she wasn't interested in dating.

But he was still always hanging around, and they ended up doing a few things as friends. She couldn't call any of those outings a date.

Maybe it was time to find out what it would be like.

She pressed her hand against his chest and gave it a little pat. "You've got yourself a date."

"Mmmmm. I like the sound of that." He curled

his fingers around her wrist and pulled her closer, wrapping his arms around her waist.

She leaned in with her lips only an inch from his. "What are you doing?"

"Being that kid in the candy store," he whispered before he planted a tender kiss on her mouth.

She melted into his strong body. Her fingers dug into his shoulders as he deepened the kiss. A soft moan vibrated in her throat. She hadn't felt this alive in years and that scared her because Edge was the kind of man she could fall for. However, she wasn't sure she was ready to give any man a chance.

Not even Edge.

She broke off the kiss and stared into his kind eyes for a reason she shouldn't trust him, but everything about Edge screamed he was one of the good men.

They were out there and she knew they existed. She'd seen it firsthand with people like Morgan, Frank, and Reese. They were all good men who would never do anything to hurt those they loved.

She blinked.

Edge ran a finger over her cheek. "I certainly didn't mind that, but you pulled away pretty quickly and now you've got this weird look. What's going on?"

JEN TALTY

"I'm sorry. This is one of the reasons I don't put myself out there." She went to take a step back, but he held her tight.

"I'm not following."

She inhaled sharply. "I get inside my head and analyze everything, and then I start thinking about what Larry did when I'm in an intimate moment and that's just never good."

"You can always talk to me about this. I don't mind," Edge said. "However, I'm not Larry. Not even close. I would never do what he did to you, and I hope you will soon believe that."

She palmed his cheek. "I know you wouldn't. I know most men wouldn't. But he made me feel as though I was nothing but a sexual object and not even the one he wanted."

"You're a beautiful woman and I'd be lying if I said I didn't want to make love to you, because of course I do." He kissed her, much like he had before. He was a master with his lips and tongue. She was lost in the moment and shivered when he stopped. "However, that's not all I want." He tapped her temple. "You're smart and kind and I want to know you. I want to learn about what makes you smile and makes your heart sing. I—"

She pressed her finger against his lips. "I get it,"

she whispered. "I've been trying to resist your charm for a long time and frankly, I'm tired of hiding from what frightens me the most."

"And what's that?"

Taking a step back, she lifted her shirt over her head. She stood in front of him wearing only his shorts.

His gaze lowered and his lips parted. His chest rose and fell with a sharp breath. He opened his mouth and shut it three times.

"Cat got your tongue?" she asked. Her smile faltered and her heart dropped to her gut. Her moment of empowerment dwindled.

"You could say that," he said with a raspy voice, hooking his finger into her shorts. "I need to know why being with me frightens you."

She took a piece of hair and twisted it with her fingers. She tried to act as if standing there with no shirt on didn't bother her, but it did, especially now that she worried he might actually say no. "It's not you I'm afraid of."

"Then what?" He took her chin with his thumb and forefinger. "Because you have to know I'd never do anything you didn't want me to, and I would never intentionally hurt you. So, whatever it is, please tell me."

She closed her eyes for a long moment. When she blinked them open, he was staring intently into her eyes. "The last time I tried to have a sexual relationship, it didn't turn out so well."

He inhaled sharply. "Did someone else hurt you?"

"No." She shook her head. "I want you. My body is reacting to you like it should. However, I'm afraid I won't be able to enjoy it, worrying about who might be watching or what might be recording."

He pressed his lips against her forehead and sighed. "If I see that asshole, I can't be held accountable for my actions," he mumbled.

She wrapped her arms around Edge. "He was my first. And obviously, my only for a long time. I have had a few relationships since then and things start out fine, even in bed, but then I get to a certain point, and all I can think about is when I walked—"

He kissed her tenderly. His hands rubbed up and down her bare back. "I don't want him in bed with us."

"Trust me. Neither do I. And it's not that he pops into my mind, but I think about the guy I'm with, and all of a sudden, I wonder what kind of porn he watches and does he watch with women, and whether he has ever been in a chat room. It's a bit of buzzkill if you know what I mean."

"I do." He lifted her off the floor.

"Whoa." She wrapped her legs around his waist as he carried her with ease toward the bedroom.

"I'm a man."

"So, I've noticed." She nuzzled her face into his neck.

He chuckled. "I've seen porn, though I can't say I watch it or seek it out because it's just not my thing, and I've never watched it with anyone. The few times I have seen it, I was alone. And you wouldn't catch me dead in a chat room. I know a couple of guys who are into that and the stories they tell totally creep me out. But if you want to know what generally turns me on, it's pretty much naked women and straight sex."

"That's more information than I needed." In the past, this was the kind of thing that would not only embarrass her but remind her of the ugliness that Larry had put her through.

He set her on the edge of the bed and ripped off his shirt, showing off his hard pecs and six-pack abs.

"You should know that you turn me on and that you're the only lady I want to spend time with and see naked. I'm kind of a one-woman man."

Tentatively, she reached out and unsnapped his jeans and lowered the zipper. She swallowed the fear that bubbled up in her gut. She had no reason to be frightened of Edge. He was kind and sweet, and any other man would have taken off running after everything she'd told him.

But not Edge.

He cupped her chin, tilting her head. "Will you tell me if I do something that makes you uncomfortable?"

She smiled as she rolled his slacks over his hips, taking his boxers with them. Her hands trembled, but she didn't care. She wanted this.

Needed it.

"I will." She took him into her hands and stroked gently. With the few men she'd been with, she couldn't bring herself to touch them intimately, creating a problem in those relationships.

Even when she had been honest about what happened and how she felt, it still ended up being an issue.

But her inability to stay engaged in sex had always been what destroyed any chance she had of being involved. And she'd thought she was okay with that.

Until now.

She licked her lips and brought him to her mouth.

He hissed. "You don't have to do that."

"I want to," she managed.

"I'm not going to complain," he said. "But I am going to ask you to stop."

She glanced up. "Why?"

"Because it has been a very long time and if you keep that up, we won't make it to this." He lay on the bed next to her, tugging at her shorts. He removed them, tossing them across the room. He cupped her breasts as he kissed her taut stomach. He fanned his thumbs across her nipples.

Moaning, she let herself relax into his touch.

He kissed her intimately. She arched her back and fisted the sheets. His tongue swirled over her hard nub while his hands toyed with her breasts, creating the kind of sensations she'd only been able to give to herself. She lifted her head and gasped as she watched him bring her the kind of pleasure that her body demanded.

Her toes curled as an orgasm built deep in her core, exploding through her system with such force her body quivered and jerked. She snapped her legs closed around his head and gripped his hair. "Oh, my God."

He kissed his way up to her nipples, taking each one in his mouth, sucking wildly. He slipped his fingers inside her and stroked until a second wave overtook her body and she cried out his name.

She grabbed his wrist. "Please stop."

"Are you okay? Did I hurt you?" He kissed her lips softly.

"God, no," she managed between ragged breaths. An aftershock rocked her middle. She shivered. "I'm...I'm..."

Gently, he thumbed her and she convulsed.

"You like that," he whispered.

"I do." She cupped his face. "I want you inside me."

"That can be arranged." He shifted. "What about birth control?"

"Oh." She froze.

"I've got it covered." He reached across the bed and pulled out a condom from his nightstand.

She watched in awe as he put it on himself. Since the incident, she found herself only wanting to have sex in the dark, and she never wanted to see anything that was going on.

With Edge, she wanted to see and feel everything. She was almost afraid she might miss something exciting if she didn't keep her focus on everything he was doing.

He eased between her legs, propping himself up on his elbows.

She arched, accepting his length. A sense of desperation crept into her mind. Keeping her gaze locked with his, she ground against him.

He matched her passion with his own desire and filled her over and over again. "Eloise," he said with a groan as he thrust into her one last time. His climax spilled over into her with such force she shuddered. He nuzzled his face into her neck, kissing her skin and whispering sweet words into her ear.

It was a good five minutes before she could catch her breath.

"How do you feel?" He pulled the covers over their bodies and hugged her close.

"Like I might want to do that again soon."

"Maybe we should stay in bed all day."

She laughed but it was cut short by the doorbell.

He groaned. "I better go see who that is." He kissed her nose. "Feel free to stay here, naked. I won't mind."

"Hurry back." She grabbed one of the pillows and hugged it.

He hiked up his jeans and stepped out of the bedroom.

She smiled. For the first time in five years, she

felt like she might actually want a man in her life again.

Ding.

A text message came over her cell. She found it on the nightstand. Larry's name flashed on the screen.

She tapped the text message. Her heart pounded. The last thing she wanted to do was talk with her ex-boyfriend.

Larry: *We need to talk. I'm outside your door. It's important.*

She bolted to a sitting position and scrambled to find some clothes. While she might trust Edge with her feelings, she didn't trust him not to punch her ex-boyfriend in the nose.

6

*E*dge rubbed the back of his neck as he curled his fingers around the doorknob. It had been over six months since he'd had sex, and that box of condoms had been bought a few months before that, but now he was going to have to check to see if the damn things expired or something because in all his years of being a grown sexual man, he'd never had one break.

When Tina had gotten pregnant, it was simply because they had been stupid kids and didn't use anything.

The doorbell rang.

Again.

He'd have to talk with Eloise about this little development, but it would have to wait.

The one negative thing about living upstairs was that Edge had to jog down the steps to see who had decided to show up unannounced.

"What the fuck?" he mumbled as he stared at asshole Larry standing on his porch, holding his cell in his hand.

Larry glanced up and his eyes widened.

"I think you might be lost." Edge opened the door and glared. He stayed in the hallway. No way in hell would he let this man in his house.

Much less Eloise's.

"Um." Larry's gaze darted from side to side. "I'm looking for Eloise. I thought she lived here."

"She does." Edge didn't care how Larry took that statement. The more he realized Eloise had moved on and he should fuck off, the better. "Why are you here?"

"I'd like to speak to Eloise."

"I don't think that's a good idea," Edge said. "Now, if you would excuse me, I have things to do."

"Wait. Is she here?" Larry asked. "And who are you to tell her who she can and can't speak to?"

"I live here too, and I don't want you on my property. So, I think it's best if you leave."

Larry narrowed his stare. "Unless Eloise tells me

to go away, you don't have the right to speak for her."

Edge inched closer. "Don't you dare tell me—"

"Edge," Eloise called from the top of the stairs.

He glanced over his shoulder. "Do you really want to see this guy?"

"Not in particular." She gripped the railing and slowly made her way down the stairs. "But I don't need the two of you puffing out your chests and starting a fight, either."

"I wasn't going to do anything but maybe escort him off *our* property." Typically, Edge wasn't a jealous man, but Larry got under his skin. It wasn't just what he'd done to Eloise that pissed Edge off. If he was being honest with himself, it bothered him that she'd actually loved this man.

He didn't deserve a woman like Eloise. Hell, he didn't deserve any lady. Not even Tamara.

Gently, Eloise placed her hand on Edge's forearm. "What do you want, Larry?"

"I need to talk with you. It's a private personal matter." He tilted his head and arched a brow.

"We have nothing left to say to one another and if this is about—"

"Eloise, please. I know you're still upset."

"You don't know shit," Edge mumbled. He swallowed. Hard. He wiggled his fingers. It had been a long time since he'd been in a fight. Since high school, actually, but his hand was itching to land right between Larry's eyes.

"I have no clue who you are," Larry started. "But this is between me and—"

"Stop it. Both of you." Eloise pulled her hair back into a ponytail at the nape of her neck. "Larry, why don't you take a seat on the porch."

"You're not seriously going to sit down with this asshole, are you?" Edge planted his hands on his hips. "You don't owe him anything."

"I know that. But I want to hear what he has to say."

"I don't trust him," Edge said. "And I don't want to leave you alone with him."

She leaned in and kissed his cheek. "Why don't you go tinker with your boat?" She pointed toward the lake. "I'll be fine. I'll yell if I need you."

He wrapped his arms around her and hauled her to his chest. He kissed her good and hard and wet. "I'm going to go put on a shirt. Do you want anything?"

She shook her head.

"I'll be right here if you need me." Edge jogged up the stairs. He did not like the fact she was giving this guy the time of day, but it wasn't his call. If he continued to act like a moron, she'd be telling him to take a hike and not Larry, and that was the last thing he wanted.

Finding his cell, he called Morgan, who picked up on the second ring.

"What's up?" Morgan asked.

"What do you know about Larry Greyling?" Edge took down a large travel mug and poured some coffee into it with a big scoop of ice. If he was going to be outside tinkering, he might as well enjoy a cool beverage.

"I've known him my entire life, but we didn't travel in the same circles. Why?"

"He showed up here today wanting to talk with Eloise and I don't like it." Edge had no idea if Morgan knew about what happened and even if he did, it wasn't Edge's place to go around gossiping about it.

Eloise wouldn't appreciate that one bit.

"They were high school sweethearts and dated into college. They were kind of an odd couple. He was so different from her, but they seemed to work until they didn't," Morgan said. "I have to admit I wasn't shocked when she dumped him. He swore he'd never come back to Lake George. He resented growing up in such a small town. But whenever he talked about their breakup, it was always about how she didn't want to commit, settle down, and buy a house close to home. I knew that was bullshit, but she never corrected his story, and it's not my place to do that for her whether I know the whole story or not."

"But he's moved back. Why?"

"I'm told because of Tamara."

"She was flirting with me last night. If she and this Larry dude are an item, she's not fully committed."

"Not necessarily," Morgan said. "Tamara's overly friendly in general."

Edge made his way to his bedroom and found a shirt. He slipped on his boat shoes. "What else can you tell me about Larry? What was he like when you knew him? Did he ever get into trouble? What kind of vibe did he give you? Anything—"

"Edge. Relax. She dumped him and she doesn't want him back."

Edge stood at the top of the stairs and pinched his nose. "I know that, but he showed up here this morning wanting to talk to her, and they are sitting outside right now."

"Are you jealous?"

"Of course I'm fucking jealous," Edge said. "But I'm more concerned. I find it strange that he just shows up back in town on the same day Eloise sits on a bomb."

"And I would agree, which is why I'm one step ahead of you."

"What does that mean?" Edge asked.

"I wanted to know more about why he was back, so I did some digging, and it turns out he's been coming into town on and off for the last three months. All to see Tamara and now rumor has it that he's looking to buy a house in the area and move in with Tamara."

"So why does he need to talk with a girl he hasn't seen in five years?"

"That is something you'll have to ask her."

"Do you believe Larry is a good guy?"

"That's a loaded question," Morgan said.

"Oh, for fuck's sake. Do you know what he did to her?"

"She told you?" Morgan asked. "I'm surprised. That's not something she ever talks about."

"Then how do you know about it?"

"We bonded over a drink a few years ago and before you go and get your feathers ruffled, no, nothing happened. She's like a sister or a cousin to me. That would be weird."

"Good to know." He rolled his neck and slowly descended down the stairs. He'd absolutely respect her privacy by barely even glancing in her direction as he made his way toward the docks. But that didn't mean he wouldn't try to listen in to their conversation.

He really had no shame when it came to protecting Eloise.

Not at all.

"Do you think I'm being overprotective and over-reactive?"

"No. I have to question why Larry would need to talk with her after all these years, so I agree, it's a bit troublesome. But there is no reason to believe he had anything to do with that bomb. Speaking of which, I spoke with Cameron. The security camera at the urgent care facility had been tampered with. There is no surveillance available for the last week."

"That's highly suspicious." That meant the facility was targeted, and likely the doctor on call. "Outside of that, was there anything worth noting on the tapes that they did recover?"

"Nothing out of the ordinary," Morgan said.

"Cameron has no solid suspects or leads. There has been no chatter regarding this bomb threat."

"That doesn't make me feel any better." He blew out a puff of air. "Thanks for all your help. I appreciate it."

"I'll keep you in the loop," Morgan said. "And Edge, don't do something stupid."

"Who me? Never."

---

*E*loise crossed her ankles and rested her hands in her lap while she focused on the boats humming up and down the shoreline instead of Larry. "I have to be honest; I don't appreciate you stopping by unannounced."

"Neither did your boyfriend." Larry folded his arms across his chest. "I texted you, but you never responded."

"Because I was busy," she said. "Now, what do you want?"

"I wanted to say I was sorry. I know what I did really hurt you, and for the last couple of years, I've been trying to come to terms with what led me down that path of destruction."

"I don't mean to be rude, but you've apologized, and I've accepted, and that was a long time ago."

"A lot has happened since then." Larry leaned forward, resting his elbows on his knees. He'd always been a contemplative man, and it seemed that hadn't changed. "Back then, I was more upset I got caught. I wasn't sincere and would have said anything to win you back."

"If you wanted that, then continuing to see that woman wasn't the best idea."

"I was pretty messed up," he said. "I just wanted you to know that I've gone to therapy. I still see a counselor. As a matter of fact, I've started seeing one in the area since I'm moving back to be with Tamara."

"I have to say I'm shocked that you and Tamara are hooking up." Eloise cringed. It wasn't her business and she had no right to judge.

"We're not hooking up. I'm in love with her." He shook his head and laughed. "Of all the people in the world, I had to run into her while on a business trip."

"You act like you resent your feelings."

"At first, I did. I mean, come on. It's Tamara. She can be a manipulative phony. But we had dinner, and she had me laughing so hard that I cried. I found out we had a lot in common and one thing led to another and here we are."

The front door opened and Edge strolled past. He caught her gaze and offered a nod and a short smile before he continued toward the waterfront. She had to give it to Edge for respecting her wishes, even though it was obvious he wasn't thrilled by her decision to speak to Larry.

"How long have you and him been together?" Larry asked.

"It's new." Butterflies filled her gut. She couldn't believe she admitted that out loud.

"He doesn't even know me, and he can't stand me," Larry said. "I assume he knows what I did." He picked at his thumbnail.

She could lie to Larry, but what purpose would that serve? "I told him," she admitted.

"That explains his hostility." Larry rubbed the back of his neck. "I hope he makes you happy. You deserve the best."

"Edge is the best," she said with pride. A little more than she thought appropriate, but she did think the world of Edge. He was the kind of man every woman wanted for herself, yet he'd chosen Eloise.

Her heart swelled. She hadn't expected to feel

this much so quickly. It scared her, but not as much as not having Edge in her life.

"You didn't come here to shoot the shit, so what do you want?" She decided it was time to find out exactly what warranted this visit.

"A couple of things," he said. "First. I don't know if you're aware, but my mom is sick. It's another reason I'm moving back."

"I did know about her recent diagnosis." Eloise swallowed the lump in her throat. His sweet mom was one of the many reasons she didn't make public the reasons for their breakup. "Her doctor is the best in the business."

"That's what I've heard," Larry said. "I appreciate you keeping the details of our issues from my mom all these years, and I was hoping you could continue to do that. At least for now."

"I don't want to hurt your mother and she's come to terms with our breakup."

Larry smiled, cocking his head. "No. Not really. Every once in a while she puts in a good word for you and it pisses Tamara off."

"I don't blame Tamara," Eloise said. "Your mom shouldn't do that."

He nodded. "I know I have no right to ask you not to say anything to Tamara, but I'm working on a way to bring her into my therapy." He lifted his gaze. "After we broke up, I went to a really dark place with some of the stuff I was doing and I'm not that same man. I really care about Tamara, and I know I need to tell her about my past and sexual addiction. I've just been afraid to lose her."

Eloise stretched her legs out and leaned back, staring at Edge while he wiped down his boat. Life had taken a huge turn and she understood not wanting to mess things up with someone. Even though she and Edge hadn't even gone out on an official date, she wanted to continue to explore what a relationship with him would look and feel like.

After years of hiding from making a real connection, a deep bond seemed to have found her and she didn't want to let go.

"If you don't want to fuck this up, I'd tell her sooner rather than later because if she finds out on her own, she'll never forgive you."

"I know." He reached out and took her hand. "I am truly sorry for hurting you."

"Just don't do that to Tamara, okay?"

"I don't plan on it." He stood, helping her to her feet. "You look good. Happy."

"I am," she said. "I hope you and Tamara make it."

"Me too." He raised his arms. "Is Edge going to beat the shit out of me if I hug you?"

"He might growl a little bit, but as long as he can see where your hands are, I think you'll be fine."

Larry laughed. "Maybe someday we can all go out on a double date or something."

"That might be pressing your luck." She gave him a quick embrace.

Edge folded his arms and glared, but to his credit, he didn't come barreling up the path.

"Take care," she said.

"You too."

She watched as Larry climbed into his fancy sports car and drove up the road to the main drag.

Edge made his way up the path and onto the porch. He leaned against the railing. "How'd it go?"

"Better than I thought it would," she admitted.

"Can I ask what he wanted?"

She nodded. "He apologized again, but this time I think he meant it. He also explained why he hasn't told Tamara about his sexual addiction."

"He called it that?" Edge rubbed the back of his neck. "Well, at least he's being open, I guess."

"He's trying," she said.

"Are you okay?"

"Actually. I'm good. Real good." She slinked

across the wood floor and wrapped her hands around his middle. She pressed her body against his and gazed into his warm, loving eyes. "How about you take me for a boat ride before I have to go to work."

"I'd love that." Edge kissed her nose. "I could pack us a lunch and it could be our first official date."

She laughed. "I don't think I've ever slept with someone before I went out with them."

"Weird, needy question." He fanned her face. "Are we an item? Because if you haven't noticed, I really like you and I don't want to share."

She dropped her forehead to his and inhaled his masculine scent. "This is going so fast."

"We can slow things down."

"I'm not sure that's possible anymore," she whispered. "And you know what I've always wanted to do?"

"No. What?"

"Make love on a boat."

"Lucky for us mine's a cabin cuddy," he said. "But we need to talk about something before we do that."

She cocked her head back. "I don't like the sound of that."

"You should know that the condom broke."

"It what?" Her pulse kicked up a notch. "Are you sure?"

"I am," he said.

"That could be a problem."

"And I think I should go buy another box since I'm not trusting those anymore."

"How about you go buy those, and I'll pack our lunch and meet you down at the dock in twenty minutes."

He kissed her cheek. "And here I thought you might freak out a little."

"Oh. I am. But there isn't anything we can do about it now." She patted his chest. "You better get going because I'm on a time clock."

7

*E*loise took out her pen and signed a few patient charts while standing at the nurses' station.

"You've had a smile plastered on your face all day," Lori, one of the emergency room nurses, said. "Which surprises me, considering you were sitting on a bomb just one day ago."

"That was an unfortunate incident." Eloise shivered. She glanced at her watch. It was pushing six in the morning and the ER had finally started to calm down.

Weekends were always filled with the nut jobs, but tonight seemed to be odder than most.

"I'd never been so scared in all my life." Eloise

placed the folders in the filing bin. "But the bomb techs were amazing."

"And what about Edge? Was he amazing too?" Lori tilted her head and batted her lashes. "I heard you gave him a nice big wet one when you came running out of the building."

Eloise smiled wider.

"Tamara's got to be beside herself. She's had the hots for Edge ever since he moved here."

Eloise laughed. "She's been secretly dating this guy Larry."

Lori leaned against the counter. "No way. How do you know?"

"Because he's my ex-boyfriend from years ago and they both showed up after the bomb scare. I was shocked to see them together, but hey, she has been acting really nice the last month. All that woman wants is to get married and have babies."

"Nothing wrong with that." Lori patted her growing belly. "Motherhood is amazing."

Eloise swallowed. She never thought she'd be in a serious relationship, much less where the thought of being pregnant wasn't the worst thing in the world. No way was she ready to be a mom, but she was ready to be with a man.

And not just any man.

Edge.

If she were being honest with herself, she'd had feelings for him for months and she'd been flirting on and off with him; however, she was always too afraid to pursue anything because she thought she wouldn't be able to get through the sex part and really enjoy it, and that's what always made her end things with the few men she dated.

"But I do worry Tamara is settling for the first man that's willing to give her what she thinks she wants," Eloise said.

"Do you not think your ex-boyfriend is good enough for her?"

"Obviously, I have a biased opinion and not necessarily in a good way for either one." Eloise had always been kind to Tamara, but she often became frustrated with Tamara's energy and her inability to read social cues. Tamara believed they were closer friends than they actually were, so when Tamara had pulled back over the last few months, Eloise had hoped it was because she'd finally gotten the hint.

Only now she realized it had more to do with her ex-boyfriend.

"I think Tamara wants so desperately to be in a

relationship, and none of the men around here that she's pursued have panned out, so she's glomming on to Larry." She wished she could say Larry was a good guy, but she didn't trust that he wouldn't be a repeat offender. Her brain kept telling her that most people who cheat would do it again if they thought they could get away with it. "But who am I to judge. If they are happy, then that's all that should matter."

"Speak of the devil." Lori pointed across the emergency room. "I don't miss working with her."

"She's a good doctor."

"Yeah. With the patients. But she treats nurses and the administrative staff like second-class citizens."

Eloise hadn't ever spent much time with Tamara in a work environment. Their shifts were always opposite each other, even when Tamara worked in the ER. She'd heard a few things from the staff both at the ER and in the urgent care facility about how Tamara didn't work well with others and being in a management position would be a nightmare.

However, Tamara did run a tight ship and other than her personality, Eloise had no complaints.

"I'm going to go find some work to do," Lori said. "I really don't want to have a conversation with her." Lori practically took off running down the hallway.

"What brings you into the ER?" Eloise shifted her stance, resting her arm on the countertop.

"I just brought Larry's mom in," Tamara said.

"Oh no. What happened?"

"She had a seizure."

Eloise had taken a break, so the other ER doctor would have been assigned to Larry's mom, but that didn't mean they couldn't switch patients. "Where is she? I'm happy to—"

"I've already had her admitted."

Eloise narrowed her stare. "She's not your patient. You can't just have someone admitted without going through the ER."

Tamara rolled her eyes. "You forget I used to work in this hospital. As a matter of fact, I was higher up on the food chain than you, and I still know people in high places."

"Are you sure it was necessary to have her admitted? Seizures are common with the type of—"

"Seriously. Just because Larry used to be your boyfriend, that doesn't give you the right to tell me how to take care of him or his family."

Eloise held her hands up. "I wasn't doing that."

"Oh, really? Then you probably weren't having a conversation with *my* boyfriend this morning while in your pajamas."

"Excuse me?" She'd known Tamara a long time, but she'd never seen this side of her before. "Larry stopped by to see me. Unannounced, I might add, which didn't go over well with Edge."

"Yes. I heard how rude he was." Tamara shook her head. "I can understand why he would have his panties in a wad, considering how he feels about me. I'm sure that was a blow to his ego."

Eloise covered her mouth, hiding her grin. Thankfully, she hadn't laughed out loud.

"But when I found out that you were pleading with him to forgive you and to take you—"

"That's not what happened." Eloise dropped her hand to her side. Anger flared in her heart. "I doubt that Larry said anything like that." She had no idea what kind of game Tamara was playing, but Eloise wouldn't participate. Nor would she let Larry off the hook. "Why don't we go clear this up right now, because I don't appreciate being accused of something I didn't do."

Tamara grabbed her forearm. "We are not going to go bother my boyfriend when he's dealing with his sick mother." Tamara pursed her lips. "You have some nerve. You can't let Larry and I be happy."

"There you are." Larry came bursting around the corner. "Oh. Hi, Eloise."

"Tamara just told me about your mom. What can I do?" Eloise would start off being kind because she truly cared about his mom. But once that pleasantry was out of the way, all bets were off.

"I think we're okay. Thanks," Larry said.

"Come on, honey. We shouldn't leave—"

"Before you go," Eloise interrupted Tamara.

"We are not doing this right now. Larry has been through enough," she said behind gritted teeth.

"Just one quick question." Eloise ignored Tamara's outburst. "Tamara seems to be under the impression that I was begging you to forgive me and that I was still interested in you, which I'm not." Just saying the words made her belly sour. "Is that what you told Tamera? Is it Larry?"

Larry closed his eyes for a moment and planted his hands on his hips. "I'm not sure what we're discussing at all."

"I didn't want to do this because Larry has enough to deal with right now, but I've got this ugly picture someone sent me of you trying to hug my boyfriend." Tamara turned her attention to Larry. "I told you that you shouldn't go talk to her. She might act all sweet and friendly, but she's had it in for me for a while now."

"Babe, besides being so lost in this conversation,

what picture are you talking about?" Larry scratched the back of his head.

"This one," Tamara held up her phone. "I've really tried to be nice to you, Eloise, but please leave me and my boyfriend alone or I'll have to call the authorities."

Eloise cocked her head. Fucking wonderful. "I can't believe you," she said under her breath. "And here I thought you changed. You can forget about me keeping my mouth closed." She snagged her clipboard and stormed off to the break room. She found a couple of dollars and bought herself a package of cookies and a soda. She plopped herself down on the sofa and let out a long breath. Her phone buzzed.

Larry: *You didn't let me finish.*

Eloise: *Does it matter? Or is she lying about how you portrayed our conversation?*

Larry: *I'm a little lost in what she's saying about our conversation. I didn't really tell her anything about it. I hadn't even told her I was going to see you. I also I haven't told her the truth about our breakup yet. I was going to do that tonight, but my mom had a seizure and that was the first time I've seen that picture.*

Eloise: *Who took that picture and why does she think I'm after you? I have a boyfriend.*

Larry: *I have no idea who took it, but she thinks you're out to get her, and I've been trying to tell her otherwise, but it's been an uphill battle and everything that could go wrong tonight, has.*

She glanced at the time.

Only six thirty in the morning. She texted Edge, asking if he was awake.

Two seconds later her cell rang.

"Hey, you," she said, letting out a long breath. "Did you sleep well?"

"Nope. Tossed and turned all night looking for you."

"That has to be one of the sweetest things you've ever said to me." She let her head fall back, and she stared at the dull ceiling tiles.

"Sounds like you had a long night."

"That's an understatement. But my morning has me ready to pull some hair."

"Do tell."

"Only if you promise not to get mad."

"That's got the hair on the back of my neck standing up," he said. "So, I can't make any promises."

At least he was honest. That was refreshing. "Tamara and Larry showed up a little while ago.

Someone took a picture of me yesterday hugging him in our front yard."

"That's not fucking possible. I would have seen someone."

"From the angle I saw the picture, it looked like it was taken from the wooded area on the side of the house. It also looks like I'm throwing myself at him, which grosses me out."

"Do you have this picture?"

"No. Tamara showed it to me when she accused me of trying to get Larry to take me back."

"I was standing right there. That's not what happened," Edge said. "Can you get me that picture?"

"We'd have to ask her or Larry for it, but it gets better." For the first time in years, she felt like she had someone in her corner. He wasn't just a new boyfriend. He was a best friend. Someone she could count on, no matter what.

She hadn't had that in a long time.

If ever.

"She thinks you're heartbroken over her and Larry."

Edge burst out laughing.

She couldn't help it. She smiled. "It's not funny."

"Well, you sound slightly amused by the statement." He cleared his throat. "She's a piece of work, but don't stress over what she's saying or even what Larry is doing."

"I have to work with her." The smell of burning toast filtered through her nose. She dropped her feet to the floor and sat up taller, inhaling sharply. "If I didn't love working at the clinic and I didn't need the money, I'd quit."

"But that's not who you are."

He certainly had that right.

The fire alarm went off, making her jump. She dropped the phone under the sofa. "Shit," she mumbled as she reached under the couch.

"Eloise? Eloise? What's going on?" Edge's voice echoed through the speaker.

"I don't know. I think someone must have burned something in the doctors' lounge, but I thought I was in here by myself." She stood and made her way to the kitchen area. "Nothing happening in here, but I smell smoke."

"And the fire alarm is going off," he said. "You need to get out."

"Sounds like a good plan."

"I'm calling the fire department now and I'll be there in thirty."

"That's silly of you..." She tried to open the door, but it wouldn't budge. "Edge?"

"What's the matter?"

"I can't get out. The door is stuck and it feels hot. Like really hot."

"Okay. Don't panic," he said with a calm voice. "The good news is that the fire department has already been dispatched. Now, who in the hospital can you text to come let you out?"

"Lori." She fumbled with her cell to find Lori's contact information.

"Don't hang up with me. Text her and if you have to, do a three-way call, but do not allow us to be disconnected."

"Okay. Okay. I sent her a text." Eloise stared at her cell, but she heard nothing back from Lori.

Nothing.

She yanked on the door again, but it didn't budge. There was no lock on the door, so she hadn't a clue as to why she couldn't open it.

"Edge. I'm scared."

"The fire department is on the way and they know you're in the doctors' lounge in the ER. I'm almost to the Northway. Morgan is giving me a police escort, so it's pedal to the metal. I'll be there as soon as I can."

She banged on the door. And banged. "No one is out there."

"Help is on the way, sweetheart. Hang tight."

Tears welled in her eyes.

"I just got word the fire trucks are in the parking lot. Someone should be at the door in a few minutes."

"What if the fire—"

"Eloise. Don't talk like that," Edge said. "Focus on my voice. It's going to be okay. The firefighters are in the building and—"

"I hear them," she said, banging on the door. "Help me."

"Take a step back," Edge said. "They are going to have to break—"

The door flung open and two first responders stood in the entryway. "Ma'am, you need to come with us."

She nodded like a bobblehead.

One of them lifted her into his arms. "I'm heading outside now," she said into the phone.

"Thank God. I'll be there soon."

"Thank you," she whispered as she wrapped her arms around the firefighter's neck. It wasn't Edge, but he'd been with her the entire step of the way. She blinked as thick smoke filled the hallways. "How bad is the fire?"

"It's not horrible," the firefighter said. "It appears

to be contained to the hallway where you were." He stepped outside and set her down by an ambulance. "But what's more worrisome is the fact that a broom wedged in the doors was keeping you from escaping."

8

*E*dge slammed his vehicle into park and shut down the engine. He jumped from the pickup and raced across the ER parking lot. "Eloise?"

She waved from the back of an ambulance.

His heart dropped to his gut. A million things had run through his mind, and none of them were good.

He crushed her to his chest and kissed her forehead. "Are you okay?"

"That seems to be your favorite question," she whispered.

He cupped her face and searched her eyes, which were filled with tears. "Are you hurt?"

She shook her head. "Just scared. It seems I might have been targeted."

Edge held her tight. "I see Cameron talking with a few of the other staff. Have you spoken to him?"

"Only briefly. He said he'd be right back."

"I don't believe in coincidences." He ran a hand across the top of his head. "If you were locked in, I'd say someone didn't want you getting out, and the last two people you saw were Tamara and Larry."

She pushed from his embrace and folded her arms across her middle. "There is no way they had anything to do with this."

"How can you be so sure?" He didn't know if he wanted to hear this or not, but he needed to respect her thoughts and opinions.

Even if he didn't agree.

Otherwise, he knew how quickly this relationship would end because she wouldn't tolerate anything except being heard.

"Larry's mom had a seizure. You can't fake that. And she was admitted."

"Please don't get mad at me, but did you verify that information? Because I don't see them out here."

She scanned the area. "A lot of people have gone back in, and they would have been on the other side of the hospital."

"Well, Cameron sent me a text just as I pulled in and while she was brought to the hospital, she was never admitted. As a matter of fact, she was turned away as quickly as she walked in."

"That's weird. I know Tamara said they admitted her," Eloise said. "I remember because I was surprised Larry's mom didn't ask for me. She usually does. Then again, Tamara had it covered, and she was being bitchy about it, so I let it go."

"So, it was Tamara who lied to you?" Edge asked. "Did Larry perpetuate it?" He didn't know who he trusted less.

Tamara was a known manipulator and she'd do anything when it suited her own agenda. But he wasn't sure what her end game was and how it tied into the fire.

That didn't make sense. She was a lot of things, but why would she want to harm Eloise?

And he could ask the same thing of Larry. If anything, he'd be kissing her ass to keep his dirty little secret.

But something didn't add up.

Eloise shook her head. "I was actually in the middle of confronting Tamara in front of Larry when the whole picture thing came up and she tried to make it sound like I wanted to steal Larry from her. Which is ridiculous." She hugged herself and made a shivering sound. "I feel like I've entered the *Twilight Zone.*"

"You and me both." He kept a protective arm around her shoulders while they sat quietly, waiting for Cameron to return. "All this weirdness started happening when Larry returned, but why? We have to be missing something."

"Why does it have to be him? What does he have to gain?"

"That's the million-dollar question," Edge said. "And we have to ask the same of Tamara."

"She's my superior at work and she has a man. That's all she's ever wanted. I don't see how getting rid of me helps her in any way."

Edge had to agree with Eloise's train of thought, only it didn't settle right in his gut.

Cameron strolled across the lot with his hands in his pockets. "We have to quit meeting this way."

"People are going to start talking." Edge stretched out his arm. "Do you have any leads?"

"I have a few," Cameron said. "The first one is we found the delivery company for the chair. Tamara paid extra to have the chair assembled. The young man who did that was tipped extremely well to perform these duties three days ago by Tamara who met him at the back entryway of the facility."

"So she lied," Edge said matter-of-factly.

"But it's her word against this kid's since we have no security footage and the kid was given cash to remove it from his books. I'm looking into that now," Cameron said. "I have lots of witnesses to the heated discussion between Tamara and Eloise this evening. I have one person who thinks they might have seen Tamara circle back by the doctors' lounge right before the chaos, but they couldn't be totally sure."

"I can't believe she'd do anything so crazy," Eloise whispered. "It makes no sense."

Edge ran his hand up and down Eloise's arm.

"From what I understand, you were both up for ER team leader," Cameron said.

Eloise nodded. "But she left the department to head up the urgent care facilities."

"Before or after you were given the role?" Cameron said.

"About the same time," Eloise said. "But she didn't want the job anyway. She likes the hours at the urgent care facilities better. Not to mention it's less crazy and less stress."

"What are you getting at?" Edge asked.

"I've talked to a few people who are under the impression that Tamara doesn't like Eloise much and that for some time there has been jealousy."

"Of me?" Eloise tapped her chest. "That's insane talk. Tamara has exactly the career she wants."

Cameron arched a brow. "Are you sure about that? Because as I've done some probing, she's had some not-so-great things to say about you to certain people." Cameron pulled out his notebook. "She said you were lazy and the only reason you got the job as team leader was because you gave sexual favors to the head of the department."

"That's gross," Eloise mumbled. "Who did she say that to?"

"A few people have come forward," Cameron said. "Morgan also learned that the kid who was visiting his underaged girlfriend next door works with Nathan as a mall cop."

"You mean that boy sneaking around in the dark the night of the bomb scare?" Edge asked.

Cameron nodded. "I had a little chat with the young man and it turns out he was hired to snoop on you and he's the one who took that picture of Eloise and Larry hugging."

"Who hired him?" Edge asked.

"He said a woman, but he doesn't know who. We

showed him a picture of Tamara and he said maybe if she had red hair since the woman who paid him wore a red wig."

"What about the bomb? Whoever did that had to have known a thing or two," Edge said. "Does that kid know anything about explosives?"

"Nathan was in the military," Eloise said softly. "He really doesn't like me."

"And why is that?" Edge pinched the bridge of his nose.

"Because I constantly refuse to give him opioids and he was at the urgent care facility the night of the bomb scare."

"I think I have enough to bring them all in for questioning," Cameron said. "You two should go home and get some rest. I'll be in touch."

"Come on. I'll drive." Edge pressed his hand on the small of her back and guided her toward his vehicle.

"What about my car?"

"We'll get it another time."

"I'm too tired and scared to argue with you," she said, resting her head on his shoulder. "I don't want to be alone."

"That's never going to happen as long as I'm in your life."

E loise opened the bedroom door and stepped into the family room.

Edge glanced over his shoulder. "You're supposed to be resting."

"I couldn't sleep." She plopped down on the sofa. "All I did was toss and turn, wondering if Nathan's behind everything or if Tamara also has something to do with it."

"I'm not trying to pick a fight, but why do you keep giving Larry a pass?"

"Because he seemed genuinely confused when I confronted him and Tamara. It was as if she was keeping him out of the loop and only playing her little game with me."

"That sort of makes sense."

"Why do you say that?" She reached out and took Edge's hand.

"Because the night of the bomb, Tamara flirted with me, but then backtracked, saying she was seeing someone. But it was definitely a mixed message."

"There was no way Nathan had enough time to assemble that bomb when he was in the facility. I checked the time stamps and he had only been there for a half hour and he couldn't have gotten back to the doctors' office."

Edge lifted his cell. "Last I heard from Cameron, he had Larry in his office, but he hadn't picked up Nathan or Tamara yet. That makes me nervous."

She tucked her feet up under her butt and rested her head on his lap. "Do we even know where they are?"

"He's got a tail on Tamara, but no eyes on Nathan."

"Why do I feel like a sitting duck?" Eloise let out a long breath.

Ding. Dong.

She jumped.

"Shit. That scared me," she mumbled.

He kissed her temple. "You stay put. I'll go see who that is."

"I hate being on edge." She pulled her knees to her chest and stared out the big picture window.

He disappeared down the staircase.

Crash!

"Edge?" She bolted to her feet and made a beeline for the door. She gasped when she saw Edge lying on the foyer floor, unconscious.

Nathan stood over him, pointing a gun at his head. "Get down here."

"What the hell are you doing?" she asked with a trembling voice.

"Just get the fuck down here or I put a bullet in his head."

Slowly, she took the steps one at a time, careful not to trip and fall. "Edge," she whispered.

"He's not waking up anytime soon." Nathan grabbed her by the hair and yanked.

"That hurts."

"Do you think I give a shit?" He shoved her toward his beat-up old sedan. "Now get in and drive toward the urgent care facility."

"Why?"

"Because you're going to get me those drugs. All the drugs."

"That's what this is all about?" As she stepped over Edge, she let out a slight sigh of relief when she saw his chest rise and fall with a shallow breath. "A bomb and a fire just to get drugs."

"I had nothing to do with the fire," Nathan said. "Now move."

"I don't understand." With a shaky hand, she pulled open the driver's side door and slipped behind the steering wheel. "Did you put the bomb in the chair?"

"Yes. That was to cover up me getting all the drugs. But you never gave them to me."

"Did Tamara know about the bomb?" Eloise eased the car into drive and headed up the private road. "Was this some kind of elaborate plan for you and her to get rid of me?"

"Aren't you the smart one." He shoved the gun in her side. "Shut up and drive."

"You're not going to get away with this," she whispered.

"Actually, I am because they will think it's all my sister. And since you're going to be dead, you won't be able to set them straight."

They remained silent for the rest of the drive. She parked his vehicle in the back employee lot of the urgent care facility. It was still shut down from the bomb scare and it was eerily quiet. She stepped from the car and tentatively made her way toward the building while he took what looked like a gas can from the building.

"Unlock the door." He pushed his gun into her back.

She groaned, fumbling with the keys.

He shoved her through the door. "Get the drugs," he said as he began to pour the accelerant all over the place.

"What the hell are you doing?"

"Making sure you can't talk." He tossed the can and held up a lighter. "Now hurry up."

With a racing heart, she did as instructed, placing as much of the medication as she could in a small bag that he'd given her.

"It's been nice knowing you." He shoved her to the floor, tossed the lighter, and closed the door.

"No!"

The room lit up with flames. The heat from the fire melted across her skin. She banged at the wood panel, screaming for help. Thick smoke filled her lungs. She coughed and slid to the floor. She swallowed and gagged. Tears burned her eyes.

This was it.

The sound of glass breaking above her head caught her attention. She did her best to scramble to her feet. The second she pushed open the door, she made eye contact with Tamara.

"What are you doing?" Eloise dropped to her knees.

"Stupid bitch," Tamara muttered.

Bang!

"No!"

*E*dge jumped from Cameron's moving vehicle.

"What the fuck are you doing?" Cameron yelled. "I can't let you run into a burning building."

But Edge wasn't about to respond. Not when flames flickered from the roof of the urgent care facility.

Sirens echoed in the distance, but they were a good five minutes out.

That could be too late.

He reached the back of the building. Ripping off his shirt, he wrapped his fist and punched it through the window.

"You couldn't leave well enough alone," Tamara's voice echoed between his ears.

He spun on his heel.

All the air in his lungs escaped as he stared at the wrong end of a gun for the second time today.

"First, your brother hits me over the head, and now you're pointing a fucking weapon at me. What the hell, Tamara?"

"What does everyone see in her?" Tamara inched closer. "I don't understand what makes her so special."

"Is she inside?" Edge raised his hands. Out of the

corner of his eye, he could see Cameron hiding around the corner, weapon drawn.

"She's going to be dead in a few minutes," Tamara said. "If you had just minded your own business, you wouldn't have to die as well."

"You're not going to get away with this," he said. The sound of the sirens grew louder. "You do hear that help is on the way."

"I do. And I'm going to be inside that building, and they are going to have to save me."

"That's the most fucked-up thing I've ever heard," Edge said.

The door fell open and Eloise dropped to her knees. "What are you doing?"

"Stupid bitch," Tamara muttered.

Bang!

"No!" Eloise screamed.

Edge clutched his gut as he stumbled backward.

"First responder down," a male voice yelled from somewhere in the distance.

Edge glanced at his hands, which were covered in blood. "I think I was shot." He blinked as he watched someone in slow motion tackle Tamara.

The sound of boots hitting the pavement pounded in his head.

"Lie back," Eloise said softly. She tore at his shirt. "We need to put pressure on that wound."

"I feel sick," he said. "And that hurts like a mother."

"I'm sure it does." Eloise took his wrist and coughed. "Are you okay?"

"I think I'm the one who's supposed to be asking you that." She waved to someone.

He rolled his head to see his fellow firefighters pushing a gurney in his direction. "Is that for me?"

"It sure is," Eloise said.

"Don't you need one?" He took her hand.

"I'm riding with you."

"Okay." He licked his dry lips. "I might take a nap, though." He tried to take a deep breath, but it hurt too much. "Did they catch Tamara?"

"Cameron is cuffing her right now."

"Eloise?"

"Yes, Edge."

"In case I don't make it, you should know that I've fallen for you."

She bent over and kissed him tenderly. "Tell me that in a couple of hours, okay?"

That was the last thing he heard as the world went dark.

9

THREE WEEKS LATER...

*E*loise rolled over to find the other side of the bed empty. "Edge?"

"In the family room," he called.

She found her robe and pulled it tight across her body before making her way into the other room.

He stood in front of the picture window, wearing only his boxers. He'd needed minor surgery to repair the damage from the bullet, but otherwise, he was fine.

She'd suffered only minor smoke inhalation.

All in all, it could have been much worse, but thanks to Larry helping Cameron put everything together, they'd been able to figure out that Tamara and her brother had been working together. Their original plan had been to steal the drugs from the facility and then blow it up with Eloise in it. When that didn't work, they went to plan B, which was to get rid of her, but the second fire had failed as well.

As criminals went, neither Nathan or his sister were very good and now they would be spending the next fifteen to twenty years in prison.

"You're up early." She stepped in behind Edge and wrapped her arms around his strong body. They had so much to talk about, but she hadn't been able to bring the one most important subject up and it shocked her that he hadn't even asked.

Of course, they had been through a lot.

"I thought I'd feel better after Tamara and her brother were sentenced, but it was a little anticlimactic." He turned, bringing her to his chest. "I feel bad for Larry. He was just a pawn in their twisted game."

"You're being awfully kind to him," she said.

"He's not the worst guy in the world."

She laughed. "I don't know how I feel about my current boyfriend being overly friendly with my ex."

Edge kissed her tenderly and with intent. "The Harmons wanted to know if I was going to renew my lease."

"I didn't know yours was up." She tilted her head and blinked. "Are you thinking about moving?"

"Kind of." He brushed some of her hair from her face. "We've been in a bit of a whirlwind these past few weeks between my surgery and Tamara and her brother copping a plea that we haven't had the chance to talk about that broken condom and if anything came of it."

Her heart hammered in her chest. She'd known the answer now for a full week but hadn't said a word in part because she was terrified he was going to freak out and run.

She stared deep into his eyes and didn't blink when a single tear rolled down her cheek.

"Holy shit," he mumbled. "I think I need to sit down."

"I've been trying to find a way to tell you, but we've had one thing after the other, and there just never seemed to be the right time."

He pulled her to his lap and rested his chin on her shoulder. "A baby?"

"I know it's crazy. But I want to have it."

"Wow," he whispered. "So do I."

"Really?"

"I love you," he said.

More tears. "This is all happening so fast, but I love you too."

He palmed her cheek. "I did something really

crazy yesterday and I called the owners of the house next to the Bateman estate."

"Are you kidding?"

"They are happy to sell, and I was thinking we could buy it. It would be a great place to raise a family."

"We're insane."

"I chase fires for a living. There's nothing normal about that." He took her mouth in a passionate kiss. "But this feels like the most normal thing I've ever done in a very long time."

"I guess we can tell the Harmon's I'm not renewing my lease either."

EPILOGUE

EIGHT MONTHS LATER...

*E*dge reached into the bassinet and rested his hand on the belly of his precious baby girl.

A daughter.

Tears burned the corners of his eyes.

She was the most beautiful little girl he'd ever laid eyes on. He loved her so much it hurt.

"Is she still sleeping?" Eloise asked.

Edge glanced over his shoulder. "Yeah." It had been a grueling labor and delivery. Twenty hours. But his wife had been a trooper. He, on the other hand, wasn't sure he'd been the best support person. He'd just come off a twenty-four-hour shift. He'd climbed into bed, hoping for a few hours of shut-eye. Eloise wasn't due for another two weeks and he figured he had plenty of time to fix up the nursery since that shift had been his last one for an entire month.

But their daughter had different plans.

He leaned over and kissed his little one on the forehead before sitting on the side of the bed. "You should try to rest some more. I'm sure that one will be screaming soon enough."

Eloise laughed. "She does have a really good set of lungs." She took Edge's hand and pressed her lips on his hard, calloused palm. "We need a name. All you could ever come up with were boys' names or dumb names."

"I'm insulted." He chuckled. But Eloise was right. He'd been adamant about not finding out the gender but had been positive it was a boy, so all he tossed out were names like Colton, River, Phoenix, and others like that. He was one hundred percent positive God would grace him with a son, because he didn't know the first thing about little girls.

Eloise constantly told him that fate would play a cruel joke if they didn't have a few female names. So, he'd suggest things like Alice, Ethel, or even Lucy, which all got him a good laugh from his wife. She told him no way was her child going to have an old lady name.

"I'm more insulted by the last girl name you offered up when the doctor announced we had a daughter."

Edge laughed at the memory. "Okay, so maybe Rosanna Danna isn't the best name."

"No, it's not." Eloise palmed his cheek as their little girl stirred. "Bring her to me. I might have the perfect name. But I want her in my arms when I say it out loud."

"All right." Edge lifted his baby girl out of the little crib. He brought his lips to her temple and inhaled that fresh baby scent. He would never tire of this feeling or of loving her and her mother. "Here you go." He placed the child on Eloise's chest. "She beautiful, just like her mama." He eased onto the side of the bed. His heart filled with more joy than he knew what to do with.

"I've thought a lot about this and the only reason I didn't say anything was because I know you." Eloise pressed her finger against their baby's lips and smiled. "You'd get weird about it, but now that she's finally here, maybe you can understand why I want to name her Tina Marie."

Edge sucked in a deep breath as the sound of his late wife's full name rolled across his ears. He swallowed. Hard. Tina had been the topic of many conversations over the course of the last eight months and he loved Eloise even more because of how she demanded Tina be a part of their lives.

It humbled him every day how much Eloise wanted to keep Tina's memory alive.

"Wow. That's a lot." He blew out a puff of air. He would always love his late wife. But he'd learned to open his heart and make room for Eloise. And it wasn't crowded. Not at all. They were two very different women. He was grateful he'd found the kind of love with Eloise that would always allow him to cherish his past, something that had always been important to him and while he did love the idea of his late wife's name, he wasn't sure this was the right way to honor her.

"I know, and if you absolutely hate the idea, I'll understand. We can find a different name." She stared into his eyes with unwavering love. "I've sometimes felt a pang of guilt for being so happy. I love you so much. You've given me the world and while I know without a doubt, you love me too. I also know we wouldn't be here if Tina hadn't—"

He pressed his finger against her lips. "What's important is that we are here. And so is our daughter, who needs a name. I'm sorry, while I love you even more for suggesting the name, it can't be Tina."

"I thought you might say that, so I have a back-up." She lowered her chin. "Christina Marie. We can call her Christina. Chrissy. Chris. Whatever you like. But Tina will always be a part of her. A part of us, which is where she belongs."

He swiped at his cheeks. "You certainly know how to make a grown man cry."

"So, do we have a name?"

"Christina Marie it is." He nodded. "Now all I have to do is figure out how to keep all the boys away because this one is never dating. Ever. Not on my watch."

Thank you for reading *Chasing the Fire*. Please feel free to leave an honest review.

If you'd like more information about Cameron Thatcher, please check out **Secret Legacy**.

Grab a glass of vino, kick back, relax, and let the romance roll in…

Sign up for my Newsletter (https://dl.bookfunnel.com/ 82gm8b9k4y), where I often give away free books before publication.

Join my private Facebook group (https://www.facebook. com/groups/191706547909047/) where I post exclusive excerpts and discuss all things murder and love!

ABOUT THE AUTHOR

Jen Talty is the *USA Today* Bestselling Author of Contemporary Romance, Romantic Suspense, and Paranormal Romance. In the fall of 2020, her short story was selected and featured in a 1001 Dark Nights Anthology.

Regardless of the genre, her goal is to take you on a ride that will leave you floating under the sun with warmth in your heart. She writes stories about broken heroes and heroines who aren't necessarily looking for romance, but in the end, they find the kind of love books are written about :).

She first started writing while carting her kids to one hockey rink after the other, averaging 170 games per year between 3 kids in 2 countries and 5 states. Her first book, IN TWO WEEKS was originally published in 2007. In 2010 she helped form a publishing company (Cool Gus Publishing) with *NY*

Times Bestselling Author Bob Mayer where she ran the technical side of the business through 2016.

Jen is currently enjoying the next phase of her life... the empty nester! She and her husband reside in Jupiter, Florida.

Grab a glass of vino, kick back, relax, and let the romance roll in...

Sign up for my <u>Newsletter</u> (https://dl.bookfunnel. com/82gm8b9k4y) where I often give away free books before publication.

Join my private <u>Facebook group</u> (https://www.facebook. com/groups/191706547909047/) where I post exclusive excerpts and discuss all things murder and love!

Never miss a new release. Follow me on Amazon:amazon.com/author/jentalty

And on Bookbub: bookbub.com/authors/jen-talty

ALSO BY JEN TALTY

Brand new series: SAFE HARBOR!

Mine To Keep

Mine To Save

Mine To Protect

Mine to Hold

Mine to Love

Check out LOVE IN THE ADIRONDACKS!

Shattered Dreams

An Inconvenient Flame

The Wedding Driver

Clear Blue Sky

Blue Moon

Before the Storm

NY STATE TROOPER SERIES (also set in the Adirondacks!)

In Two Weeks

Dark Water

Deadly Secrets

Murder in Paradise Bay

To Protect His own

Deadly Seduction

When A Stranger Calls

His Deadly Past

The Corkscrew Killer

First Responders: A spin-off from the NY State Troopers series

Playing With Fire

Private Conversation

The Right Groom

After The Fire

Caught In The Flames

Chasing The Fire

Legacy Series
Dark Legacy
Legacy of Lies

Secret Legacy

Emerald City

Investigate Away

Sail Away

Fly Away

Flirt Away

Colorado Brotherhood Protectors

Fighting For Esme

Defending Raven

Fay's Six

Darius' Promise

Yellowstone Brotherhood Protectors

Guarding Payton

Wyatt's Mission

Corbin's Mission

Candlewood Falls

Rivers Edge

The Buried Secret

Its In His Kiss

Lips Of An Angel

Kisses Sweeter than Wine

A Little Bit Whiskey

It's all in the Whiskey

Johnnie Walker

Georgia Moon

Jack Daniels

Jim Beam

Whiskey Sour

Whiskey Cobbler

Whiskey Smash

Irish Whiskey

The Monroes

Color Me Yours

Color Me Smart

Color Me Free

Color Me Lucky

Color Me Ice

Color Me Home

Search and Rescue

Protecting Ainsley

Protecting Clover

Protecting Olympia

Protecting Freedom

Protecting Princess

Protecting Marlowe

Fallport Rescue Operations

Saving Love

Saving Magnolia

Saving Leather

Hot Hunks

Cove's Blind Date Blows Up

My Everyday Hero – Ledger

Tempting Tavor

Malachi's Mystic Assignment

Needing Neor

Holiday Romances

A Christmas Getaway

Alaskan Christmas

Whispers

Christmas In The Sand

Heroes & Heroines on the Field

Taking A Risk

Tee Time

A New Dawn

The Blind Date

Spring Fling

Summers Gone